Praise for *Swimming with Dead Stars*

"Vi Khi Nao is an absurdist dreamer with a lacerating view of the world and its ills. *Swimming with Dead Stars*, a philosophical treatise on adjuncting, illness, and relationships, is ferocious and alive, like a monstrous field of technicolor flowers foaming at the mouth."

—Patrick Yumi Cottrell, author of *Sorry to Disrupt the Peace: A Novel*

"Vi Khi Nao's *Swimming with Dead Stars* teems with bodies—corporeal, celestial—churning and circulating, beating, and always costing: money or time or relationships. I felt each word of this book, so potent, bury itself inside me, and I buried myself inside Nao's text, became entirely a part of her world. It's that powerful."

—Sarah Gerard, author of *True Love: A Novel*

"All of Vi Khi Nao's books share a mythopoetic impulse and create together a world in which modes of being and art-making seem suddenly more recognizable in their elaborately evoked never-before-seen-ness. Nao reminds me of Antoine Volodine, not stylistically, but in her forging of genres that seem distinctly her own."

—Joanna Ruocco, author of *Dan*

"Maldon is a very human character even as she is also celestial, mineral, elliptical in her orbit."

—Sarah Blackman, author of *Hex: A Novel*

SWIMMING WITH DEAD STARS

SWIMMING WITH DEAD STARS

a novel

VI KHI NAO

FC2

TUSCALOOSA

Inquiries about reproducing material from this work should be addressed
to the University of Alabama Press

Book Design: Publications Unit, Department of English, Illinois State
    University; Director: Steve Halle, Production Assistant: Pearl Osibu
Cover Design: Matthew Revert
Typeface: Baskerville

Library of Congress Cataloging-in-Publication Data is available from the
Library of Congress.
ISBN: 978-1-57366-193-5
E-ISBN: 978-1-57366-895-8

for S.A.

"Does the soul wear a feather dress?" God

"This was not the result of carelessness or of lack of knowledge, but of downright resistance to the mere possibility that there could be a second psychic authority besides the ego. It seems a positive menace to the ego that its monarchy could be doubted." C. G. Jung's *The Undiscovered Self*

"Ali is retiring his tail from circulation." Far Wall's *Phrenzy*

THE LAW OF MALDO-NISM: a) Not to be surprised. b) We give ourselves too much credit by believing too much in the law of synchronicity. c) I am here because I haven't been here before? Things only appear to happen suddenly because you have been in denial for so long. d) You think you can die, but you can't.

THE LAW OF NEPTUNO-NIAN: a) Why are you here, planet Neptune? I am here so that you may see that I have always been capable of instability. b) A place where you could understand what it is like to always live inside of a greenhouse effect. The consciousness is always breathing under the atmospheric condition of hydrogen, liquid ammonia, methane. And now you know. c) You are moving, Earth, in the same frequency as my existence, and now you sort of orbit me until you sort it all out. d) Most planets gaze at each other with some disease of distance. Since I am here, this is my disease with you. e) When nonfiction becomes obsolete, it becomes fiction.

code:

Sun = ☉

Moon = ☽

Mercury = ☿

Venus = ♀

Mars = ♂

Jupiter = ♃

Saturn = ♄

Uranus = ♅

Neptune = ♆

Pluto = ♇

PROLOGUE:

"You are the Sun. The Sun doesn't move. This is what it does. You are the Earth. The Earth is here for a start, and then the Earth moves around the Sun. And now, we'll have an explanation that simple folks like us can also understand, about immortality. All I ask is that you step with me into the boundlessness, where constancy, quietude and peace, infinite emptiness reign. And just imagine, in this infinite sonorous silence, everywhere is an impenetrable darkness. Here, we only experience general motion, and at first, we don't notice the events that we are witnessing. The brilliant light of the Sun always sheds its heat and light on that side of the Earth which is just then turned towards it. And we stand here in its brilliance. This is the Moon. The Moon revolves around the Earth. What is happening? We suddenly see that the disc of the Moon, the disc of the Moon . . . on the Sun's flaming sphere, makes an indentation, and this indentation, the dark shadow, grows bigger . . . and bigger. And as it covers more and more, slowly only a narrow crescent of the Sun remains, a dazzling crescent. And at the next moment, the next moment—say that it's around one in the afternoon—a most dramatic turn of event occurs. At that moment the air suddenly turns cold. Can you feel it? The sky darkens, then all goes dark. The dogs howl, rabbits hunch down, the deer run in panic, run, stampede in fright. And in this awful, incomprehensible dusk even the birds . . . the birds are too confused and go to roost. And then . . . Complete silence. Everything that lives is still. Are the hills going to march off? Will Heaven fall upon us? Will the Earth open under us? We don't know. ☽ — János Valuska[1] from Béla Tarr's *Werckmeister Harmonies*

[1]https://www.youtube.com/watch?v=_d5X2t_s9g8

♀

After placing a sixteen-quart pot onto the first burner to make *canh khoai tây cà rốt sườn*, she was out of breath. She had informed Rebecca Curtis and Walter Benjamin that she was deteriorating. But what did this mean? She got tired easily; after walking four steps, she felt like she had run a marathon. She got out of breath easily, as if someone thought she was leftover dinner at The Olive Garden and Saran-Wrapped her face in plastic, choking out her life. She would have welcomed all of this if it weren't for the existence of her mother. For as long as she still existed, she planned to ban her mother from attending her funeral. But she was here in Su 890, sitting under the bright Sun, inside, experiencing a sinful kind of paradise under the heavy guidance of antibiotics in her system. She had left the entire East Coast, her students at Westerlund, her luggage to a beautiful young man with nine fingers, and her former lover in New Jersey, her pink handbag purchased when she was in Mexico City, and a bag of gluten-induced oats. In another strainer and then into the big pot, she is steaming sweet white and red Yukon potatoes and these purple Peruvian fingerling potatoes that look as if they have gangrene or some fancy form of bacterial infection that obstructs circulation. Venus, the planet, texted her:

VENUS: How was the Moon last night out there?

MALDON: I did not see her. Did you on your end?

VENUS: A fat cut of butter.

MALDON: The moon is going to give you high cholesterol if you bite too much into her.

VENUS: I accept. I can always run it off.

MALDON: Immorality isn't for everyone.

VENUS: Not for everyone. How has your jaw been, Maldon?

MALDON: Better—the antibiotics are helping.

VENUS: Even the Sun wants to take a bath in a swimming pool of dead stars.

MALDON: No, I just want to make butterfly strokes with dead stars.

VENUS: Forgive me, you still plan to have the surgery, yes?

MALDON: Yes.

VENUS: Do you like to swim in pools of water?

MALDON: No. I get tired too easily. The weight of water. The amount of newtons my heart has to exert.

VENUS: The natural end of an arc before it becomes a star. What planet would you like to be?

MALDON: I would like to be someone's umbrella.

While the deep-violet fingerlings were steaming without their planetary umbrellas, she thought resentfully about her trust fund, overachieving students, and the ineloquent director who stood by them. The director, who hadn't made time to introduce Maldon to Westerlund, decided finally to force a meet-up at a Korean restaurant across from campus, which, subsequently, gave her diarrhea afterward. The director came because a cacophony of complaints had ambushed her inbox, and she felt compelled by the force of her directorship to address them. There was no place for coats.

DIRECTOR: I would have loved to treat you to lunch, but I have gotten myself into debt.

MALDON: . . .

While fussing over the menu, the director opened lunch with an apology, the kind of apology that made Maldon feel immediately impoverished, as if she had lost something or someone stole something from her and then immutably, after the robbery, announced to her that she had, indeed, intentionally stolen it for effect. Maldon understood that the director's apology was more about expressing her emotional hoarderness and not necessarily about the director being paid poorly (she wasn't paid poorly), nor about generosity without proper compensation, as who needs, ever, compensation for adjuncting or labor exploitation, nor about the unaffordability of a $15 meal. So, why did the director start out with an apology when she was the director, after all? Was this about diplomacy or about the misdistribution of power? Perhaps everything near and in between. Maldon briefly glanced at the director and understood. Long before this conversation was to take place, the administrator had informed Maldon that Maldon did indeed have full authority over her own classroom and that she had the autonomy to set rules and standards for the classroom's limited structure. Already the director was planning to remove power from her—first through an apology, then, as the conversation progressed, through guilt, and if guilt didn't do the job, she would resort to fear. Maldon stared ahead into the unattainable future of the afternoon. From the glass panels of the restaurant window, she felt the emptiness of the clusters of snow. It had been falling in big splashes as if snow were a child, a little girl wearing rain boots who didn't mind stomping her legs with each stride, announcing her grand presence in a world designed for pointlessness and well-exercised nepotism. She studied the boulevard of gallimaufried jewelry draped across the director's whitening skin and thought, you could afford all of that gaudy décor and you couldn't afford to treat your hired, underpaid literary object who had just flown across half the state to teach your class? The charitable prandial digression might have developed some un-ignited passion in her, had her appetite for life and food been remotely semi-colossal, but, alas, for the last month or so, since her well-accepted, pre-invited abduction here, Maldon had lost her desire to eat, and each second of her existence had been about her non-existence. Even if the director felt decently marvelous and even humanly possible and had treated Maldon to a meal, she would have felt some degree of repulsion for such a contestable prospect. Maldon realized that she hated her, and there was simply no language for this hate.

Each day was a battlefield. To exist or not to exist. Simply, Maldon did not want to exist. She studied the fat splatters of snow spitting at everyone who dared to get in their way and turned her gaze back toward the menu. There was nothing she wanted, but Westerlund wasn't giving her much of an option. She asked for something cow-y with rice. And, later, when the Korean waitress delivered the goods, it tasted terrible. Like it sat too long near a bathroom stall while trying to get in line to take a beefy piss. She hated the director. And the more the director opened her mouth to dispense, to piss out the complaints her students had written, overflowing her inbox, the more she felt part of her being reappointed. There was nothing here on the East Coast for her. It was becoming apparent to her. The hours spent on the lesson plans—she quickly abolished them from her mind and decided that her students were lame and that this director was even lamer. Maldon half-heartedly listened. She watched the director move her salad around while fate began a different thread of conviction for her. Because the temperature wasn't dropping fast enough, the snow would retain its fatness, and the circumference of its corpulence would continue to widen its heliotropic diarrhea. Maldon studied the soft, institutionalized snow and realized that their lunch was nearly at an end. Soon they would enter this semi-frozen vapor party. Her shoes would soon be soaked and caked with salt, dirty snow, and street grime. Maldon's mitral heart felt heavy. Before leaving the restaurant, while they were still moving salad (white) and rice (colored) around, the director had informed her that, just across the street, a student had committed suicide due to extreme academic stress. The ominous, unmarked site of the student's death still permeated the consciousness of Westerlund's population, and students were still learning to cope with this tragedy. In her stupid defense of the lame students who were exhausted and burnt out from four years of institutionalized classes, and in realizing that she was losing a specious battle with the unknown, the director had shifted into the fear-inducing aspect of her argument to thrust her point forward.

DIRECTOR: The intuition and its current structure are stressing the students. They simply don't know how to cope.

MALDON: ......

Maldon read between the lines, and, within seconds, she lost her respect for the director. Everything would be downhill from this point on. The director's anti-pseudo-suicidal reasoning would have gained more ground if the instructor wasn't suicidal to begin with, but to threaten and mildly blackmail a suicidal instructor was like bringing a gun into a gunfight and expecting to be at an advantage, especially if the gunwoman was slow at drawing. Lack of work ethic, though appearing dressed as if there were a lack of time, compelled the director to apply the fear card to garner power over the situation. But the situation was doomed from the start. There was nothing wrong with Westerlund or its instructional structure. One can't simply blame the institution for our malnutrition of ethics. We are helpless, but not that helpless. Soon, the snow would stop snowing, and the air couldn't be fat anymore, and hyperventilation couldn't become a man-made source of obesity objectification.

Since she didn't have cash with her, and the restaurant allowed only one credit card per transaction, Maldon Venmoed the director $15.00. The transaction was swift. Though behind the wallet of politics, there was something understated and dirty and ugly about the exchange. They both walked briskly toward the gate while stomping the snow into pre-blizzard submission. Lunch cost Maldon $15 and a stomachache quite unnecessarily, but it cost the director a lot more. The director would unravel this costly gift within a month. Meanwhile, the director asked Maldon about her health, and Maldon casually mentioned that her health had depreciated. She intentionally downplayed its gravity. Maldon downplayed the depths of her suicidal convictions, her life-threatening illness, and the exponential rate at which she was deteriorating. Maldon understood that the director was no friend of hers and would treat her accordingly. They parted ways. Maldon was forced to spend her evening near a bathroom stall. The bathroom on the sixth floor always seemed to be occupied, and she found herself using the broken sewage system on the fifth floor.

When she finally took the elevator up to the sixth floor, Maldon found herself face-to-face with the administrator. The administrator relayed to her that she had recently been on the phone with the director.

ADMINISTRATOR: You are a genius, she said!
MALDON: . . .

Maldon understood that the director had a sixth sense that the conversation had not gone well; overindulging her with compliments was her way of coping, of seeking balance. Words, though cheap, based on personalized empirical data such as false positive reinforcement, gave the director the fastest key to perform damage control—easy come, easy go—words she realized had a high success rate of adjusting the equilibrium of a person or a quarrel. It was the equivalent of feeding sugar to post-diabetic patients in hopes that the diabetes would go away. Maldon rejected everything. She didn't care if the director thought she was a genius. She did wonder why the director used this tool of manipulation to solve difficult problems. Major problems in life generally cannot be resolved with verbal candies. Then Maldon felt sorry for the director. She knew, standing in that office facing the library while snow fell in large clumps and the plants standing tall pressed their verdant hair and wept silently against the glass pane of the office's jungle climate, that her time at Westerlund was coming to a complete stop. She may be dying (cardiologically and psychologically), but Westerlund was an inappropriate sarcophagus for her soul.

The appropriate catacomb? Possibly the following burial mounds:

> Margarita with Maldon
> Negroni with Maldon
> Mojito with Maldon
> Martini with Maldon
> Moscow Mule with Maldon
> Sidecar with Maldon
> Vesper with Maldon
> White Russian with Maldon
> Screwdriver with Maldon
> Bloody Mary with Maldon

Maldon sea salt was born and bred in 1882: coastal, continuous custodians of a primordial gastronomic ritual, crystalline pyramids of taste, recognizable by its town. Maldon knew early on that if her life hadn't been destined to be pinched and crushed by thumbs and fingers, she would have been a fisherman. She has been told over and over again at cocktail bars how her existence has enhanced the life quality of bartenders and cocktail rims alike. When she is pinched, she feels like she has woken up from a snowflake of a dream.

Contemporary life is brutal. Existing is brutal, thought salty Maldon. Weeks before, an editor and friend of Maldon's had informed her over Thai food in Brooklyn, not too far from the Greenpoint bookstore, that everyone at Westerlund bites their nails and pulls each other's hair to get an adjunct teaching position at Westerlund. All along, Maldon had thought that New York had a shortage of teachers and they needed to plug someone from pastoral, bovine, in-the-middle-of-nowhere Cloud for the position and Westerlund had had no choice but to ask heart-wrecked Maldon to do the job. When she saw the director disappearing into the snow with her flamboyant coat, she thought what a terrible decision she had made, bringing her wrecked body here. And for what? Fat snow? Lectures on workload? Whatever? She had made a mistake flying here. Would she ever forgive herself? Her body was certainly berating her for it. She had studied the squinted nose of the director and had felt sorry for herself. People kill each other for so little. When the snow melted, the salt left behind on her convalescent body stained her, almost made her rusty, overoxidized, and discolored. She spent most of her time in a Brooklyn apartment staring at the ceiling and the ceiling fan. And then life took over. Her interviewer, Venus, carried jugs of water to the edge of her apartment for her and drove her to Seven Lakes Drive, about an hour or so north of the city, near Bear Mountain, where she cried because she had become too aware of her life coming to an end. The wind sent mini-catastrophic debris across her face, lambasting her with its gelid smites whenever she took her soul outside to buy oats, apples, and cannoli. Once in a while, she would buy one yogurt and eat it over three days.

Venus had taken her on frequent night drives around the Upper West Side, always stopping by the edge of The Cloisters to study the shadows and hidden gothic atmosphere of the nunnery turned museum.

MALDON: When spring arrives and the leaves come out to play, visit The Cloisters, Venus. Smell the poisonous plants in the garden. But don't eat them.
VENUS: I won't eat the poison.
MALDON: Wise of you.

Maldon had always preferred the horizontal life over the vertical. Sitting and standing took too much effort. Her weak heart didn't have to work so hard to pump blood. She lost consciousness less that way. She even felt like she might not lose her liver that way.

Then she recalled being on the phone with a literary agent who had a remarkable British voice that sounded like a water lily looked—the aquamarine kind, with a concealed doorknob in it. The doorknob may look like Anne Rice, though she was uncertain.

MALDON: My literary career has been a salad spinner.
AGENT: I see.
MALDON: All the broth is falling out of the holes.
AGENT: And you want to retain it.
MALDON: Will you help me keep the broth in?
AGENT: I will try my best.

MALDON: Do you know the Iraqi-British architect, Zaha Hadid? Her radical deconstructivist buildings?
AGENT: Yes.
MALDON: I want to be the Zaha Hadid of literature.

Perhaps the British agent couldn't hide Anne Rice in her door-knobbed lily. Maldon thought how much she loved having suicidal thoughts. How her world might have a definitive ending as opposed to a novel, which seemed to have endless possibilities. When life didn't try to morphine-drip her with sumptuous photos of well-groomed food, she felt totally wrecked by the possibility of famous people. A decade or so ago, she read somewhere that Jeannette had fallen in love deeply, perhaps even convinced the married woman (was she married?) with curls or without curls to live with her forever—and then not too long ago Maldon read somewhere that they broke up, and Maldon recalled being fairly distraught by the news. She wasn't entirely sure what provoked her or what it was about Winterson that made her deserve marital happily ever after, but Maldon felt betrayed. If Winterson couldn't afford to live happily ever after, what were the chances for Maldon? It was true she didn't care about God or the interior lives of God, which is what humans were designed for: to showcase God's gaudy shoulder pads, warm modernism, site inspections of patterns, commercial human hoteling of elbows, myopic tongues in the decorative industry of upholstery, armpit hair well-furnished for theorists of the ninetieth century, rib bones chased down by chinoiserie furnishings and Elsie De Wolfe, and dark torsos fringed with dolphin wreaths. Then Jupiter, the planet, wrote her.

JUPITER: Do you want to be a spine-chilling, antiquated futon?

MALDON: Is it a cobalt-blue futon?

JUPITER: I don't know. It has indigo porcelain arms.

MALDON: Seal me in wax, please.

JUPITER: Windheld me to you.

MALDON: Do you mean "windshield"?

JUPITER: Windhold.

MALDON: What is that?

JUPITER: Last night I dreamt that I time traveled. Space folding within itself. It was with a man I have never met before. We were walking toward this infinity pool, and he told me to plunge in, and when I did, my body floated out to space. I did not need gears or wear an astronaut suit to survive. He was telling me how time can easily bend into itself. Not like an origami figure but like a piece of paper. Later, another man approached me. He remembered me because he had seen me seconds ago in an alternate universe. He pretended that we had never met before. But he knew I had time traveled.

MALDON: Windhold you to time. I will do just that.

Yesterday, Maldon's mother divided her *canh khoai tây cà rốt sườn* into small food storage containers. It only took her mother four hours to contain the containers and for the containers to contain the four-hour-breathing broth. Then Maldon went for a desert walk without her mother where the wind spoke louder than its acridity, and she felt forced to return home because the allergies, the awoken pollen, the dull, uneventful flowers were having an eventful party inside her nose and eyes, and whenever she secreted sweat, desire, or liquid mucus, she felt like a plant that just watered itself. Maldon had always believed that she was a desert plant of some sort, belonging to the Joshua tree family, but she was learning very quickly that she was closer to rose mallow, cranberry bush, even summer sweet and hibiscus. Then there was the inkberry theory.

MOTHER: What is an inkberry theory?

MALDON: A shrub that isn't susceptible to disease.

MOTHER: I am your mother.

MALDON: Perennials, mother. All of my shortcomings are perennials.

MOTHER: I won't deny that.

MALDON: And low maintenance

MOTHER: Like the inkberry.

MALDON: Not in theory. Only architecturally.

MOTHER: What is architectural psychotherapy?

MALDON: It's when you build buildings so that form follows function. Ecologically. Psychologically.

MOTHER: If all of my psychological issues were form in architecture, then does it follow that they have practical uses in modern life?

MALDON: Give me an example, Mother.

MOTHER: When we adopted you, we were fully exercising our theory in abandonment.

MALDON: Mother, architecturally and psychologically speaking please.

MOTHER: We gave you an outhouse. Form follows function.

MALDON: Because I was adopted—

MOTHER: Yes, you were susceptible to diseases at a young age.

MALDON: Psychological diseases.

MOTHER: Boanthropy.

MALDON: What is that?

MOTHER: Rare.

MALDON: How rare?

MOTHER: You thought you were really a cow.

MALDON: I was raised in Cloud, farmland and kernel hypnotism.

MOTHER: Thank god, it was short-lived. We knew. Because we adopted you, we had to realize that you were not entirely from our herd.

MALDON: Did I eat grass?

MOTHER: Like a wolf.

MALDON: Wolves don't eat grass.

MOTHER: Sure they do.

MALDON: Let's talk about the outhouse.

MOTHER: It was good for you, until your great lover Klüver-Bucy came for you.

MALDON: Who was she?

MOTHER: Klüver-Bucy syndrome.

MALDON: Oh no.

MOTHER: You could have been sexually attracted to any inanimate object, like a rice cooker or a barbecue grill or night table; and I would have understood. But noooooooooo!

MALDON: Oh no.

MOTHER: Maldon, the outhouse? Really?

MALDON: My god, Mother.

MOTHER: Your medial temporal lobe was fucked up. What was I supposed to do?

MALDON: Un-adopt me.

MOTHER: You wanted to be intimate with the doorknob of the outhouse. You took your pink shovel and you shoveled piles of shit out of the outhouse into the rice cooker.

MALDON: Shit. Shit. Shit.

MOTHER: You conveniently had amnesia afterward.

MALDON: You conveniently love me.

MOTHER: I conveniently love everything I touch.

The outhouse experienced low aggression with Maldon, but its docility made it difficult for the two to experience separate anxiety, especially after some urinary release where the forest may have been. Maldon's mother believed that the two Parkland teens who survived the New Zealand shootings had committed suicide because they loved the government too much, when their love should have been devoted to outdoor architecture such as an outhouse. When the shootings occurred, Maldon was at the ER at St. Luke's, just a few blocks from the main gate of Westerlund.

MALDON: Sydney Aiello.

MOTHER: . . .

MALDON: What's the other girl's name?

MOTHER: Still a juvenile. Her name is undisclosed.

MALDON: If only these girls spent more time making love to an outhouse, they may have found reasons to live.

MOTHER: I'll pretend that I didn't hear that.

MALDON: Do you think Aiello was high on magnesium?

MOTHER: What is your point?

MALDON: Do you think she wanted to turn her body into ammunition?

MOTHER: Bullets are generally made of lead, copper, metal . . . .

MALDON: I love how she was a female bullet made entirely of magnesium.

MOTHER: Her mother might think otherwise.

MALDON: Do you think I would be good at oral sex?

MOTHER: Have you tried stuffing four goldfinches into your mouth at once?

MALDON: Some of them were nonbreeding males . . . . Do they still count?

MOTHER: If they are bright yellow enough, maybe.

MALDON: I think I'm better at oral history.

MOTHER: Tell me about Saturn eating his children.

MALDON: Worried that one of his progeny would oust him from the throne after his wife, Ops—

MOTHER: Better name for her would be Oops—

MALDON: As soon as Oops gave birth, Saturn (her husband) would immediately devour his own child.

MOTHER: Such unnecessary ferocity. Couldn't he just kill them?

MALDON: Feasting is a more active way to annihilate.

MOTHER: Where was the mother in this?

MALDON: When the third child came into the world, she substituted him out. She wrapped a sheathing of non-him in stone.

MOTHER: A veteran cannibal couldn't distinguish flesh from a rock?

MALDON: Mother, he was full of madness. His reasoning wasn't all there, you know.

MOTHER: But still . . .

MALDON: Demented, I would still know if I were eating a few baby fingers or a lump of cobble.

MOTHER: Are you sure you aren't good at oral sex?

MALDON: How do you define good?

MOTHER: Three goldfinches in the dark.

MALDON: And when it's not dark?

MOTHER: Two goldfinches and a parrot.

MALDON: You want a penis that emulates the human voice?

MOTHER: Well, it wouldn't hurt . . . .

MALDON: To have something arrestingly colorful.

MOTHER: Down there, reminding you to fuck .

MALDON: It's time for me to serve you some British tea.

MOTHER: Gunpowder, please.

MALDON: What about Maghrebis?

MOTHER: Gunpowder in a casket, please.

Maldon served her mother liquid gunpowder with Sydney Ai-ello in a small casket called a teacup (with only one handle) to make the unremarkable vocation of the pallbearers easi-er. When her mother placed the gunpowder onto her liquid tongue, Maldon squirmed a little to the left. Not too unlike a slug or whelk. Inhumation was not a shared function for her. She preferred shared humiliation. When she was in high school, a group of young boys followed her home from school and mocked her Vietnamese by pronouncing English words out of it. Maldon preferred being humiliated this way: she knew the boys were attracted to her, and they were catcalling her, forcing her to eat their crows. Whenever crow's-feet appeared near her eyes, she recalled the ferocious nature of their uncontrollable, priapic, gastropodic appetite and how she made them swallow their own slug by turning around and shouting, "Your penises looked like eggrolls that have been poorly wrapped by Clint Eastwood." Whenever her father served her these fried male genitals of the Asian persuasion dipped in fish sauce, she thought the universe had a very odd sense of humor. Whenever her family rolled these and sold them for $2 apiece at the farmers' market during the inebriated days of college football Sundays, the Cloud farmers were so copulatorily gay. They kept swallowing these Asian swords and moaning. Their gustatory lips glistered with a mixture of dark vegetable and canola oils. Now, with a broken tooth, she found it difficult to chew anything, let alone a six-inch saber made from shredded cabbage and carrot, wheat flour skin, ground pork, and vermicelli noodles. In the early morning, Venus wrote Maldon.

VENUS: How do you feel today?
MALDON: In pain.
VENUS: What does it feel like? Like a casino sleeping on top of your heart?
VENUS: I have since leapt from the horse's burning eyes.
MALDON: Yes, let that horse seduce you.
VENUS: Please take the painkiller. You'll need it for the root canal.
MALDON: I know my face well.

VENUS: I can see your quiet face trying to bear the pain.
MALDON: I learned a long time ago that language is about
           submission.

It was true the inkberries had been crushing her soul. And she
wanted to commit suicide very badly. There were simply no
painkillers for psychological pain. How to kill herself while her
mother was still alive? The quandary of not existing continued
to upset her and forced her into a hellhole designed solely for
self-preservation. A can of olives. Two cans of persimmons. A
half a dozen of spam. Tomatoes bathed in high sodium content. Albino-colored baby chickens married to botulism and
toxins that cause respiratory failure and indigestion and paral-
ysis. Self-preservation made her think of canning her life. Was
extending her life a way of canning her existence? What about
hydrating her life? Is there a way to exist by ceasing to exist?
The longer she self-preserved, the more she felt like those cans
of preserved food that Cormac McCarthy's post-apocalyptic
protagonist in *The Road*, played by Viggo Mortensen, seemed
to push about in his rattling, gut-wrenching shopping cart. At
the dentist's office, she thought how ironic it would seem if she
spent $450 she did not have to laser-whiten her teeth. Or if
the dentist performed the most beautiful root canal on tooth
#18 and then she hung herself using a belt on her mother's
fiancé's bathroom door. Wasn't this the most ideal way to exit
this world? The only travesty about this beautiful watercolor
painting of her existence was that she did not own a single
belt. Famous folk who committed suicide via fancy or unfan-
cy drapery: Kate Spade, Alexander McQueen, Bhagat Singh,
Hideki Tōjō, Robin Williams. Fancy draperies may include:

cummerbund, girdle, strap, sash, *cinture*, clout, bind, bang, bal-
dric (oh, why not). She wanted to be a one-time expert in the
art of carotid artery compression, the twisting of the jugular
region, the cul-de-sac to the human lungs. She also wanted to
break her spinal cord. It wasn't something one could experience every day, but suicide made all this possible.

MOTHER: Maldon.

MALDON: . . . .

MOTHER: Maldon.

MALDON: What is it, Mother?

MOTHER: Get ready. We must go now.

MALDON: I thought lunch wasn't until noon.

MOTHER: Get dressed.

MALDON: It's only ten a.m.

MOTHER: Still.

MALDON: Does he know that we don't live in the same
          apartment?

MOTHER: I'll tell him ten minutes before lunch.

MALDON: Why not now? So he has time to adjust his
          arrival.

MOTHER: I don't want him to know where we live.

MALDON: Okay, Mother.

MOTHER: Did I tell you once that his friend died in his
          car when he was picking him up from the air-
          port?

MALDON: He just dropped dead on the ride home while
          they exited McCarran Airport.

MOTHER: So you remember me telling you. How terrifying
          it must have been for him.

MALDON: Tell him to pick me up next time from the airport.

MOTHER: He's a good driver.

MALDON: Mother, you used to date him. Of course, he's an amazing driver.

MOTHER: He used to be a chef.

MALDON: Does he have a lot of burn scars on his body?

MOTHER: He's very careful.

MALDON: But still . . .

MOTHER: He's really good at eating sushi.

MALDON: All men like to say that.

MOTHER: He was very attentive.

MALDON: To the sushi or to you?

The place where they ate served French, semi-Italian/Mediterranean cuisine. Quite vexingly, they served no jasmine or sushi rice. And the restaurant wasn't emotionally capable of providing *bánh bèo* (literally "water fern cake") and certainly not northern-style *phở*, and forget about *gỏi cuốn* (summer spring roll), and a Hội An dish called *cao lầu*. However, they were potentially and psychologically capable of preparing such things if Southern California placed an AR15 against the temple of one of the chefs. What was she supposed to do? Ask post-pyromaniac California to do the impossible task? Her mother ordered hummus and a burger to share with Maldon. Her mother's ex ordered a panini. Dining warfare happened when rice paddies go to war with durum wheat. It was a war no one could win. In her mother's and her mother's ex's world, eating sushi was a coded language, like a fancy military language for eating pussies. The dentist told her after the root canal operation to only consume soft food. What was soft on the plate? Hummus?

AARAV: I'm so sorry about your diarrhea!

MOTHER: Was it the hummus?

MALDON: My internal Boeing 737 MAX plane made an emergency landing near the American Paris sewage system.

MOTHER: What food is French?

AARAV: It can't be the hummus.

MALDON: Did they spray the lettuce with E. coli?

AARAV: We should ask them.

MOTHER: Just to be sure.

MALDON: Food poisoning isn't my best friend.

MOTHER: It's nobody's best friend.

MALDON: Unless one has been tortured through scaphism or "the boats," a Persian torture method in which the tortured is placed into a concave tree or empty boat and forced to imbibe molasses or corn syrup through the human orifices: throat, asshole, vagina—and kept alive until the tortured died from septicity or infectivity.

AARAV: What about the ants, bugs, visitors of four, eight, twelve, twenty legs?

MALDON: What about them?

AARAV: I am asking—

MALDON: Unless I participated in an unceremonious torture activity, how would I know?

AARAV: The ants and insects are morally clueless.

MOTHER: What they have been consuming has been born

from torture.

AARAV: I think they are incapable of knowing.

MOTHER: They know.

When the monarchic orchids arrived without the gnats, hornets, beetles, and other arthropodal beings, Maldon sobbed into their regal bodies and wiped away her tears with the spine of Joseph Conrad's *Typhoon*. She knew a tropical storm, the opposite of dehydration, was always wet and incapable of decreasing the liquidation of her tears, but she had nothing else to wipe her face with. Everything else, such as the water bottle, the candleholder, and the lighter, seemed to be clueless, like the arthropods, about decreasing her sorrow. Was it true what Gaston Bachelard stated in his *The Poetics of Space* that "wolves in shells are crueler than strayed ones"? Was it true that she did not want to live anymore?

Meanwhile the daffodils were arriving from the sea of grass into the Westerlund campus. And, in an office overflowing with plants, flowers, and desire, a woman gathered her ginger shredder, a tea ball strainer with a chain around its neck, and a teacup made specifically for nomadic mouths and leaned back into her chair to contemplate the cherry blossoms which would stop hibernating in their floral core to greet her near the gate of the university. They had a new instructor this week. Finally, they would get a normal, fully functioning instructor who could properly give them the kind of pedagogy they needed and deserved. She supposed that her imminent departure was a gift. Since the beginning of her class, they had been wailing for a normal instructor, and now that they were getting what they wanted, she wondered

if they were happier. Life was too short to be chronically dis-
satisfied.

When she descended the stairs to urinate, she noticed the rice
cooker. It was sitting alone on a table, being very micro-comically
quiet and demure. She wondered if the coffee maker ever felt ag-
itated or infuriated with it and spit a spoutful of coffee at the poor
porcelain rice cooker. These inelegant thoughts arrived without
permission or authority. It vexed her—this other dimension of
life, coughing up dimensions that acted more like philosophical
irritants than the conscious pleasure of things being things. She
wished life would just fuck off and leave her alone. Nanosecond
by nanosecond, atom by atom, photon by photon.

Her mother's man came home after being a commercial truck
driver for Walmart. He worked one week and had one week off.
During his one week off, when he entered their apartment, he
tried his best to manspread his existence as much as he could.
He would turn the TV on at full volume and sit for hours watching Netflix. Every four hours he would announce his hunger by
farting, and Maldon's mother would feel compelled to make him
a meal. She cooked him Paula Deen's southern-fried chicken in
which all the chicken fat looked like it had gone to war with
The Man with the Yellow Hat or the entire continent of In-
dia. Maldon would always feel so bad for her mother. Her own
lack of financial freedom prevented her from giving her mother
her freedom. Maldon spent years trying to "rescue" her mother
from the travesty of indentured slavery. In terms of minimum
wage, at least a sex worker got paid more than her mother. Maldon had been trying to teach her mother how to outsmart her
man, but her mother had not been too compliant.

MALDON: Ask him to start a joint bank account with you.

MOTHER: He doesn't want to give up his power that way.

MALDON: Each time he gives you money to buy groceries.

MOTHER: I know it's only one or two hundred.

MALDON: Maids get paid more than that, and they don't even have to cook. And they get tips.

MOTHER: It's a relationship.

MALDON: Then why does he pretend to give you the illusion of chivalry?

MOTHER: By asking if he could help.

MALDON: It's called performance chivalry.

MOTHER: I know.

MALDON: Where it *sounds* chivalrous but is not chivalrous.

MOTHER: I know.

MALDON: Mother.

MOTHER: Daughter.

MALDON: If he deposits money into a joint bank account and you use such resources to cook food for both of you, it's part of shared domesticity.

MOTHER: He gives me money.

MALDON: That's what is devastating, Mother.

MOTHER: What is?

MALDON: It looks as if you owed him services or resources or gratitude because he gives you money for services rendered that benefit primarily him! Forcing you to feel indebted to him for the gift of one or two hundred dollars. With a shared bank account, the illusion of indebtedness will vanish. So that grocery money doesn't become a form of indebtedness for you. When he gives you one

	hundred or two hundred dollars, the physical transaction of money seems—
MOTHER:	Pornographic. I know.
MALDON:	Relationships trap us financially, Mother.
MOTHER:	I know.
MALDON:	They trap us psychologically so that we never climb out of our enslavement.
MOTHER:	What can I do? I lost my entire retirement savings. *I have nothing.*
MALDON:	You have me.
MOTHER:	But you're so poor.
MALDON:	I am wealthy in so many other ways.
MOTHER:	I am so tired of him sitting on his ass and then offering to help. Empty words.
MALDON:	And he just stares at the screen!
MOTHER:	Is my life like a garden salad?
MALDON:	I'm teaching you how not to micromanage me.
MOTHER:	Why is that?
MALDON:	So that you can be more successful.
MOTHER:	I heard Steve Jobs loved to do that to his subordinates. Look at how successful he was.
MALDON:	When you micromanage people or your daughter, it limits you.
MOTHER:	In what ways?
MALDON:	A large part of success is calculated trust.
MOTHER:	That's what micromanagement embodies.
MALDON:	No, mother. Micromanagement is overcalculated distrust.
MOTHER:	Same thing.

By the time she climbed the stairs into her convalescent room, Maldon was ambushed with a ubiquitous ickiness. It took her no time to discover the source of her ickiness. She rushed quickly into the bathroom, yanked down her pants, and there it was: God's plan for her existence. It was her third period within the month of March. How many periods did God have in mind for her body? If she didn't want more, how could she retaliate? If she allowed the Sampha song to climb into her soul, would it alter God's multi-directional impulses for her period? Dying was an exciting event for her. She wanted to die. So badly. Three weeks ago, on the morning that she taught at Westerlund, her heart was racing at an obscene 150 to 200 beats per minute. In a pre-fainting and pre-fading state, she packed up quickly, almost in a military style, all her possessions on the East Coast. She packed in seconds. Everything layered into her suitcase. Her breath was fading. Later, she described her heart as a mouse with its rubber ball (her heart) unlatched, slipping out of its socket. When it slipped out, she knew death was dressed in camphor, clamoring for her existence. She knew it was time to die and she welcomed it. She was not afraid to forego her promise to remain alive for her mother.

MALDON: Take me, death.
GOD: You will leave her alone.
MALDON: Ignore him, Lucifer.
GOD: You will leave her alone.
MALDON: Please give me permission to die.
GOD: Permission denied.

Didn't God declare that "It's easier to ask forgiveness than to beg for permission?" And then there was that Sampha lyric leading his seductive rose back to her, "No one knows me like the piano in my mother's house." And then her heart slipped back into its own dress and returned to its normal beat of 70 per minute. Just like that, she did not slip away and did not die. Ever since that day, she frequently found herself standing for five minutes in front of the TV, the refrigerator door, the kitchen sink, the washer and dryer, in shock at her own existence. Shock that she was still alive. She grieved as if she had lost something mammoth and monumental. When the disappointment of being alive settled in, she realized that God was teaching her an important life lesson: her will to die had to be perversely more powerful than God's will for her to live. Although God won this time, she knew it wouldn't be long before she would eventually win. Dying is not an art, Sylvia Plath. It's a gurney on a journey.

When she descended the stairs after refusing to participate in the third episode of her ovulation cycle, she found her mother's man sprawled out on the sofa. His short stubby legs looked like tree stumps recently chopped from the forest. Maldon wanted to throw his zaftig legs into the fake fireplace. The fireplace was fake; its invisible mouth was made entirely of glass and gave the illusion of a fire. Modern life in Su 890 taught her that warmth was about asking the emperor to wear all of his new clothes without the mirror being his mistress.

MOTHER: Look at him.
MALDON: I can't believe that thing asked you to marry him.
MOTHER: It usually takes him two or three days of behav-
                   ing like a zombie to get back to his normal self.
                   You must sympathize.

MALDON: Complacency is what ultimately kills, Mother.

MOTHER: Not if lethargy and exhaustion get to us first.

MALDON: It's no excuse for him to treat you like a live-in maid.

MOTHER: He is financial security.

MALDON: Are you sure? You don't even wear the eight-thousand-dollar wedding ring he gave you.

MOTHER: It reminds me too much of concentration camps in Cambodia.

MALDON: You used to swallow and poop out your wedding ring every day. For a month.

MOTHER: Your father didn't care.

MALDON: About the poop or about your nuptial anniversary?

MOTHER: He didn't really care.

MALDON: I know he never replaced the one you sold to get us out of that persecuted place.

MOTHER: Our exile and arbitrary detention.

MALDON: I remember that large ship.

MOTHER: Yes, I had to kick that woman so she would make room for you near the bow of the ship.

MALDON: We made it out of that concentration camp.

MOTHER: Not entirely in one piece.

MALDON: I remember how dry it was.

MOTHER: Despite us being so near the equator.

MALDON: It wasn't scalding.

MOTHER: But we were quite destitute.

MALDON: Mother, how did you find the will to get us out of there?

MOTHER: I bargain with hardship.

MALDON: You make it impossible for me to end my life.
MOTHER: If I knew . . .
MALDON: Let's try it sometime.
MOTHER: Let's include your brother. He has been trying.
MALDON: We all have been trying . . . .
MOTHER: And not succeeding.

The administrator at Westerlund Skyped her into her office to announce how her absence was making the entire English building weep. Maldon wanted to be an emotional hoarder of something, but she was distracted by the desire to mow the lawn. Over digital pixels, Maldon studied the administrator's facial structure: regal and strong with a hint of briny, nautical Nairobian ache or despair. She introduced Maldon to the Russian professor dressed like Julia Child who was to take Maldon's place in teaching Maldon's class. The video call was visually sharp, no disruption nor poor connection. Her lover, Earth, texted her afterward.

EARTH: I know you don't have a *New York Times* subscription, but I'd love for you to read this piece by Nicole Dennis-Benn called "Who's Allowed to Hold Hands."
MALDON: I just read it. It's heartbreaking.
EARTH: It puts in words what I know and have experienced. The violent reaction of black men toward black women. The ache of wanting to just be and to express my feelings with my lover in any space. The constant censorship. The cost could be our lives.
MALDON: Is it as costly as suicide?

I think everything is costly.

To breathe is costly.

To exist is costly.

To love is costly.

I don't think the pain of existing is worth the cost.

Would you rather hold hands and die or live and not hold hands?

I want my death to be quick and efficient.

Maybe the best way to commit suicide is to hold the hand of the woman I love?

EARTH: You're a romantic or a pragmatist.

MALDON: My next nonfiction book will have this pending title: *How to Write About Suicide While You Are Still Alive.*

EARTH: It's hard to write about suicide if you are dead.

MALDON: It's kind of hard.

EARTH: Maybe it looks harder than it really is.

MALDON: Looks can be deceiving.

EARTH: Deception isn't hard.

MALDON: It's harder than it looks.

EARTH: It's easier than it seems.

MALDON: Even far away—

EARTH: Even from far away you make me feel less lonely and taken care of.

Existence called her by her fucked-up name. Existence here and existence there. Existence everywhere. Maldon's period bled into the night, soaking up four pads within five hours. Their wings wilting into soggy bogs of deep red embarrassment.

Each time she rushed into the bathroom, she felt like a pitcher of uterine sangria sweating ruby through its vermillion base. It leaked into her underwear and pajamas. She changed underwear four times within one day, gingerly waiting for the female cycle to wring existence into a load of washing. The rest of her day unraveled feverishly. Bleeding so much within a short period had shifted her face into a new shade of green, almost like a ginkgo leaf that had acquired new eyes, wearing red-rimmed glasses and shifting un-sturdily into the wind. When she climbed back upstairs to change out a new pad, her energy level unthreaded frivolously and in the heat of this frivolity, she noticed her mother sprawling out on her yoga mat. She had arranged her petite body into some un-deranged, uncomplicated posture, maybe like the muscular shape of the letter L, the lower part of the L being her mother's short back. Her long legs hung in the air in a straight line. Poor Maldon believed right then and right there that she was doomed. At the healthy rate her mother was living her health-conscious life, she was going to live forever, which meant that Maldon's plan for suicide had to be postponed, rescheduled for another decade or two or three. At the rate her mother was surviving, eating so well, exercising so meticulously . . . Maldon's state of mind began to hyperventilate. She pulled down her pants, and cochineal flowers bloomed one after the other in between her legs. How could she commit suicide if her corporeal, eco-friendly mother kept on living efficiently and competently? Was there a better way to die than waiting for her mother to die? Speechlessly, Maldon got the sense that she was too ontologically disorganized. She needed a better business plan for dying. Her short-lived entrepreneurial endeavor needed corporate backing.

What corrupt institutions of being were willing to fund, hasten, and accelerate her death? Her original business proposal had been that her heart would start to break down in five years. She wouldn't need her heart to be operated on. No surgeries. At the age of 45, she could die a natural death. As she told her students, she wanted to walk toward a tree one evening in the summer, lean into a mulberry tree, and lay down to die. This would buy some time for her mother to experience more of old age, give her mother some time to advance her death by vanishing in her sleep one day sometime in the next five years. She didn't want her mother to suffer. Not perish from breast cancer or kidney failure or leukemia. And certainly not from Alzheimer's. She hadn't expected her heart to deteriorate, for her valve to malfunction so quickly, for the soil to knock on her door, demanding that she seek medical attention nippily and urgently. Also, she found herself lying and being dishonest quite quickly, which was out of character for her. Maybe it was deceit that made it okay for her to exist. To continue lying. Her friend from the East Coast wrote her thoughtfully.

ASAHI: Please don't die, Maldon.
MALDON: I will try not to.

Which was a real lie. She had been trying to die. She felt terrible for her friend. To compensate for her deception and to weaken, etiolate her guilt, she said something melodramatic and nostalgic about their previous dinner outing together.

MALDON: I'm happy we ate at the Peruvian restaurant. You gave me really really good chocolate.
ASAHI: I'll give you more good chocolate if you survive.

MALDON: Yes, great incentive to live.

ASAHI: So survive. I will make you more sangria.

MALDON: With grapefruit?

ASAHI: Yes.

How hard is it to die? thought Maldon. It would seem assholic to Asahi if she told her that she wanted very much to die and just didn't know how to go about it. She rhetorically asked herself silently: when is deception a good thing? When you kill yourself without telling anyone? Or you kill yourself without giving any warning signs? To make it worse, her lover from the East Coast was making grand efforts at decreasing the counterfeited value of reality by being warm and affectionate.

EARTH: I've started my period in solidarity. I can't still be linked to you, right?

MALDON: My god.

EARTH: Yes, we must still be tethered.

MALDON: This life.

EARTH: I'm perimenopausal and rarely have a period. So this is not a normal artifact.

MALDON: My body is trying to abduct yours.

EARTH: And my body seems willing to follow. It's a conspiracy.

MALDON: Your body could retaliate.

EARTH: It's old enough to know when it's time for sweet surrender.

MALDON: Is it truly sweet?

EARTH: I'm going to take a break from all that surrendering to get you a hot water bottle, cool cloth for your head, and a foot rub.

MALDON: My god.
EARTH: At your service, my lady.

Her mother, her mother's fiancé, and Maldon had lunch. In the middle of a very rushed lunch, Maldon's fiancé asked to be excused from washing the dishes. He wanted to ride his motorcycle to Big Sur. Her mother became irritated. She wanted to enjoy a slow, elongated lunch where all three of them could relax and languish in the unclenched afternoon of the last day of the workweek. But he left. Rushed out the door as soon as the last pocketful of rice leaped into his mouth, forcing her mother to both prepare the meal and close it.

MOTHER: I never want to marry.
MALDON: I understand.
MOTHER: Not to that. That rushed life. That rushed body.
MALDON: He can't help himself.
MOTHER: Did you not notice that I said nothing?
MALDON: That's who he is.
MOTHER: I told him that we are going to the library. So when he asks—
MALDON: I know what to say.
MOTHER: What will you say? You must prepare ahead.
MALDON: I know what I must say.

Her mother was coaching Maldon on how to lie properly. Sitting in her mother's car in the passenger seat with the window rolled down, Maldon attempted to sleep, but the feverish chill and menstrual ache, pain, and profuse bleeding were making her ill and exhausted and irritable. She sat in the car while waiting in the garage of her mother's friend's house because she was feeling terribly cold on one of the warmest spring days in Su 890. As if she were a salamander and the car was the warmest rock on which she could sunbathe her small, icy frame. Her mother was sitting in her friend's garage in front of a sewing machine with piles of her belongings stacked high behind her like random claustrophobic products displayed in the largest outdoor shopping factories in third world countries such as Mexico, Vietnam, or Zimbabwe. Her mother hadn't wanted to move in with her fiancé. She didn't want to lose her freedom and she didn't want to marry him, but she didn't have an income or a place or of her own, so out of desperation, she moved in with him. To trick her mind into thinking it was just a temporary transition, her mother only moved in the few things she needed to exist: clothes and cosmetics. Her mother was hemming a pair of jeans and a black evening dress for her client. Both of the items needed to be completed that evening. With the car's foldable sunshade blocking her view of her mother, the extreme heat of the car sedating her, Maldon considered the dishonesty construct: when someone exposes our lies, are they asking us to find a new way to lie or reinvent a new way to tell the truth through another innovative method of lying? Do we ever stop lying? Do we continue to lie and become dishonest and not know it? We may know it peripherally. We don't ever stop. Lying, that is. Just as Maldon realized that she was helping her mother with her dishonesty, lying with her, thus also participating in the lie and therefore lying herself. By realizing this, she believed she could be exempted from the lie, but in fact, if she was honest with herself, she was lying through intimate proximity, which may be one of the worst ways to lie because this lie gave her the brief, delayed notion that her sin of turning a blind eye or tongue, or her gesture of nonchalant omission made her impervious to the lie because she felt that by refraining from saying anything, she was not actively participating in the lie: lying with some distance or lying through the arm-length methodology. When we lie this way, we actually lie more casually and more frequently because the lies don't seem as harmful or egregious, and so we allow ourselves to participate in the lies more habitually. Lying with knowledge and awareness is worse than lying without, because we know better and yet refuse to behave in accordance with that indispensable law of knowledge. But lies, like compounded interest, are just as deadly and dangerous as carbon monoxide or slow poisoning. Is this solidarity dressed as deception or something else? Maldon thought. Maldon could have told her mother's truck-driving fiancé that her mother didn't actually go to the library. Her mother, in fact, needed to go to her friend's place to have access to her sewing machine in order to work on her customer's clothes. She actually didn't have a storage unit in Su 890. Before moving in with her fiancé, she had asked her friend of a decade if he would allow her to stash her belongings in his garage. He agreed. Maldon had an epiphany: she realized that when we don't lie, our success lasts longer because it is truer and more authentic. When we lie, we are pseudo successful: we seem to get what we want in the moment, but it is only temporary. As soon as our lies catch up to us, our lies make us pay, make us accountable for our wrong or our wrongdoings. The truth saves time, and it is the most accurate portrait of our most current and updated evaluation of reality. But we don't choose this method because we are sometimes lazy and human and complacent. We can become arrogant and demand things that we don't truly deserve. We want more than what we need, and we become greedy with the things we don't have or must have.

If she hadn't helped her mother participate in the lie, she could have stayed home and rested in the comfort of the bedroom provided for her. She could rest her terribly fraught body and give it the kind of serene affection and consolation it craved. Instead, she was sitting in a car to stay warm to help her maintain the façade of her deception. She felt a chill crawling around the different pockets of her perspiring pores, forcing her to feel overwhelmingly exposed to the disease of that dishonesty. Should she betray her mother by telling her fiancé that they didn't actually go the library? What is the best gateway to honesty? What was the best way for her to stop lying with her mother without betraying her mother?

Then Mars, the fourth planet from the Sun, texted her.

MARS: Maldon, you.
MALDON: You terrestrial planet. You thin atmosphere.
MARS: Yes, me, all red and iron-y. Irony! Get it? Get it?
MALDON: Oh, fuck me.
MARS: Fuck you?
MALDON: Well, not in the ass. Any rate, you are—
MARS: What?
MALDON: Not well-equipped to fuck anyone.
MARS: I don't have the instrument.
MALDON: You don't.
MARS: Ah, I get it.
MALDON: I am thinking about solidarity.

MARS:	What kind?
MALDON:	The kind where women commit suicide together.
MARS:	This old world fucked by men, run by men.
MALDON:	That's right.
MARS:	Suicide doesn't solve things, right? You know that, right? Look at all the dead stars.
MALDON:	In biblical times, the oldest child of each Egyptian household (except for those with red marks on their door) was willed to die. If every single woman in every household commits suicide and the world experiences a high population of maternal emptiness, men will be forced to change.
MARS:	Are you sure this is the best way for women to un-enslave themselves from men?
MALDON:	Pharaoh released the Israelites, didn't he?
MARS:	Well, he had a moment of relapse and came chasing after them.
MALDON:	Like I said, the best way to make it matter is to stop existing. It may seem counterintuitive, but extinction has its value. Dinosaurs knew this very well.
MARS:	Man, that's what the Red Sea is for.

She watched while the world went on without her. Her agent originally had a flyer with her name on it. And now she saw the same flyer by chance on Instagram. She saw the flyer, but her name on it was gone. Her name had been substituted with another's, and just like that her existence was replaced. Just like that she stopped existing. Is suicide like that? One day here and the next gone? Her name no longer on the flyer of life? Was this how God generally advertised existence? As if in retaliation against God, she went to her agent's Instagram page and un-liked all her likes, which was a lot. She had liked nearly all their posts. Just like that she was slowly erasing her digital carbon footprint. If she repeated this blanket gesture on all sectors of her life, how many years would it take to erase herself from existence?

After a night of sleep, Venus texted her.

VENUS: Your heart, Maldon, how is it? Still waiting to see?
MALDON: My heart is still waiting for its doorbell.
VENUS: Would you like that doorbell to work?
MALDON: I like soundless doorbells.
VENUS: How does that work?
MALDON: I don't really know yet.
VENUS: By the way, how was the sockeye salmon you prepared for your mother?
MALDON: My mother thought it was very good. I guess I know how to cook.
VENUS: A noble skill to possess.

Without her family knowing, she was hoping to die on the East Coast, her body shipped back to Cloud for burial. Instead, here she was still breathing, still helplessly existing. Here she was existing almost against her will. Though there was no mario-netted force maneuvering the strings of her being, nonetheless she felt something imposing itself on her. A few weeks after she nearly died, a Russian translator bumped into her while she tried to take the 1 train into Brooklyn.

TRANSLATOR: Hey, you.

MALDON: Have you ever been in a terrible accident and then, instead of dying, you wake up, and both of your femurs are broken, your nose crushed, your face mauled like a blood-soaked paper towel? You have just catapulted through three windshields. One kidney is missing. Your arms bent like a clothes hanger. Your throat slashed. Your chest and neck should have been tattooed red with a seat belt. A few of your toes are missing

TRANSLATOR: That's terrible.

MALDON: You call God up and you tell him to take you.

TRANSLATOR: I see. When he doesn't take you, you feel like you just woke up to a terrible accident.

TRANSLATOR: Tell me about the heart operation.

MALDON: No.

TRANSLATOR: No?

MALDON: No.

She left the translator at the platform.

Her brother phoned her from Cloud.

BROTHER: Tell me about your heart operation.

MALDON: What do you want to know?

BROTHER: Everything.

MALDON: No driving for four weeks.

BROTHER: I'll drive you.

MALDON: Eight weeks of lifting nothing more than five
                    pounds while the breastbone heals.
BROTHER: We will buy a forklift to help you lift things.
MALDON: Okay.
BROTHER: You might die.
MALDON: I might.
BROTHER: You might need a blood transfusion if something
                    goes wrong.
MALDON: I might.
BROTHER: They are going to insert a long, hollow tube through
                    your groin so they can inflate your heart.
MALDON: And you need dental clearance.
BROTHER: No bacteria in your mouth.
MALDON: Because bacteria tends to stick to the heart valve.
BROTHER: Right.
MALDON: The surgeon is like Mom.
BROTHER: How so?
MALDON: A seamstress. She is going to use an Ethibond
                    thread to sew a mechanical valve to a ring.
BROTHER: Well, it's not a pig's valve.
MALDON: What if—
BROTHER: You can't eat pork anymore.
MALDON: No reversal of blood flow in my pulmonary vein.
BROTHER: You almost died on the East Coast.
MALDON: Did I tell you what the doctor said to me?
BROTHER: What?
MALDON: Nothing.

After her mother's fiancé took them to a fancy buffet at a casino in the middle of nowhere, near a remote desert, they all

went shopping. They stopped by Macy's, then Dillard's, then more stores. After stores. Maldon was wiped out from the pure gesture of existing. Her mother had selected some soft clothes for her to try on. She briefly studied her body in the mirror. She couldn't believe that in a few weeks a scar the length of a foot would travel like a wounded zipper from the center of her clavicle to her belly button. It seemed so surreal to her. The surgeon breaking her breastbone with a surgical hammer in order to have access to her heart. Though it was more likely that they would take a bone cutter to break the center of her body into accessible parts. Then, probably with a salad tong, the surgeons and their staff would dig in, pulling some kale and olives and human salad dressings from the salad bowl of her body. To replace her valve, they would insert a small mechanical bicycle wheel into her, just in case her left breast wanted to take a short ride down to her kneecap; if it did, it would have the right transportation to do so. The surgeon said she could choose between an organic wheel or one made out of metal. The semi-self-regulating mechanical wheel had the unfortunate condition of being able to last forever, meaning that she would need to be on Warfarin or some other kind of blood thinner for the rest of her life to prevent any blood clot. If a blood clot occurred, it meant her bicyclic-like valve would experience obstruction and wouldn't work so well and would ultimately stop pumping blood in and out of her heart properly. A malfunctioning valve would mean she had a chance of dying, which excited her greatly. An organic wheel was made of tissue and had an expiration date of about ten years, which meant that in ten more years, if she were still alive, she would need another valve replacement. The entire operation would take a total of six hours. The surgeon had told her that her anterior and posterior leaflets were thickened so badly that they couldn't be fixed, which felt like a white lie to her though she had no empirical data to back this intuition up.

She wanted her brother to overhear the conversation she had with the surgeon. But she simply didn't know how to get him to be a part of it.

MALDON: Would you leave a cellphone inside me?

SURGEON: No, I would be laser focused during the entire operation.

MALDON: What would distract you?

SURGEON: I would be laser focused.

MALDON: But would you?

SURGEON: They don't allow cellphones in the operating rooms anymore.

MALDON: Would you try to call me?

SURGEON: I wouldn't. It would be hard to without a cellphone.

MALDON: I noticed there is a phone booth on the fourth floor of this hospital.

SURGEON: Yes.

MALDON: I think it's coin operated.

SURGEON: You are telling me this because . . . ?

MALDON: So you bring quarters with you before surgery.

SURGEON: I pay for things in Benjamins.

MALDON: What do you mean?

SURGEON: I just think surgery should be performed on white people. They have a higher chance of living longer and they don't mention any presidents before the Eisenhower era. The mortality rate for immigrants is so low. Terribly low. At any rate, I have other patients I must see.

Maldon didn't think this doctor was very smart and wondered how the woman had made it through medical school and performed surgery in the last five years or so. On the other coast, she heard her planet Earth getting ready for the next day, searching her bedroom and drawers for workout clothes, her black bras, and packing lunch. She heard all of this vibrant, monotonic life over the cellphone. It all felt strangely comforting.

Someone else living a life. Just being and existing. Could she choose a life where she just exists? Simply exists for the sake of it? Was such a life possible for her? This auditory life on the other side of the world. Somewhere in New Jersey a woman was going to bed really late. She could hear the radio static of her existence. The ambient white noise of her corporeal movements as she packed her life for tomorrow. Across the cellphone line. One lifeline over the other.

MALDON: You must sleep. I am going to be here tomorrow.
EARTH: I am not sure about that.
MALDON: You are not sure?
EARTH: I am never sure.

Now her planet Earth was sitting in a chair, relaxing. Not going to bed. "It shouldn't be too cold tomorrow," Planet Earth informed her.

MALDON: A lot of my work took place in my heart. Took place in my mind. It is a good thing you don't see me deteriorating so fast. I don't have the heart to tell my mother how fast I am deteriorating.

And so young Maldon carried herself well. Trying to hide her own tiredness, her excessive bleeding from her mother. She couldn't hide it from Planet Earth, who over the phone could hear her breathing heavily just from existing.

MALDON: It is nice that you are going to miss me when I am gone, but even if you don't, it's okay too.

EARTH: I am going to miss you when you are gone, Maldon. Plain and simple.

Long silence between them. The empty zone. Where she could hear her own voice ringing. She venerated her lover for not trying to convince her to live this life. She admired her. Her voice rustling like a tree branch.

EARTH: What do you want?

MALDON: Nothing. I need to write my will. A will shouldn't take that long. To write.

EARTH: What do you want?

MALDON: Nothing.

EARTH: Someone almost always wants something.

MALDON: Either it is the beginning of my life or the end of it.

EARTH: Today I spoke to the mother whose daughter died. In my old country, her sister died when she was five years old. Just five years old. The mortality rate so high. She was so little when her sister died. Now she has died and before she died she was in so much pain.

MALDON: It must have been so hard for you to watch her being in so much pain.

EARTH: It was.

MALDON: What are you doing not being in bed?

EARTH: I am just sitting here.

MALDON: Just sitting. That's beautiful.

EARTH: You know why?

MALDON: Why?

EARTH: To do that British thing.

MALDON: I see.

EARTH: When the daffodils come out in the spring, I read the daffodil poem. In our country we don't have daffodils, but the British forced it in our education, and we would read it even though we don't have daffodils in our country.

MALDON: Did you forget to?

EARTH: I did. I did, Maldon.

MALDON: Would you like me to read it to you?

EARTH: Yes.

MALDON: "I wandered lonely as a cloud/ That floats on high o'er vales and hills,/ When all at once I saw a crowd,/ A host, of golden daffodils;/ Beside the lake, beneath the trees,/ Fluttering and dancing in the breeze/ Continuous as the stars that shine/ And twinkle on the milky way,/ They stretched in never-ending line/ Along the margin of a bay:/ Ten thousand saw I at a glance,/ Tossing their heads in sprightly dance./ The waves beside them danced; but they/ Out-did the sparkling waves in glee:/ A poet could

> not but be gay,/ In such a jocund company:/
> I gazed—and gazed—but little thought/ What
> wealth the show to me had brought:/ For oft,
> when on my couch I lie/ In vacant or in pen-
> sive mood,/ They flash upon that inward eye/
> Which is the bliss of solitude;/ And then my
> heart with pleasure fills,/ And dances with the
> daffodils."*

A few tears traveled down Maldon's face as she read the poem. In the early morning Maldon had interviewed a poet in Nor- mandy, but two hours into the interview, she became etiolated, wiped out as if she had run a 10K marathon, despite sitting and resting. Her day had been clumsy. The hour felt an hour off. It seemed so surreal. She was so excited. For the first time she wanted to be selfish. She wanted to pack her life for death. She had tried it once on the East Coast, packing everything in five minutes.

EARTH: It's obvious. You are what you are.
MALDON: I am such a minimalist.
EARTH: You even tried to minimalize your life by ending it.
MALDON: You asked me to record what I packed the day I thought I died.
EARTH: Let's see it.
MALDON: I took a picture of it.
EARTH: Even better.
MALDON: One half or partly eaten Divine seventy per- cent cacao dark chocolate with ginger and

---

* William Wordsworth

orange; one ovoid tea strainer; one nail clipper with a diary key (diary missing); one pink and one gray comb; one gold shoe-shaped ashtray made in Pakistan; one thin, elongated plastic lipgloss with black cap; one small pocket sanitizer; one elongated travel-sized perfume bottle; one L'Oréal makeup kit containing one 4TB external hard drive and US passport; one circular yoga tea box made to counter insomnia, complete with a cotton drawstring bag; one pair of black Bang & Olufsen earplugs and accompanying protractor-shaped black case; one small vial of liquid ginger; five sexy Victoria's Secret lingerie pieces in a Ziploc bag; one MacBook Pro charger; one summer dress dyed pinkish lavender; one light lavender-colored maxipad; one $10 bill; two $5 bills; one Frida Kahlo journal purchased in Mexico City; one Nature Valley Crunchy Oats 'N Honey Granola Bar; one pair white Samsung earplugs; one parabola-shaped ginger root; one travel-sized verbena lavender hand lotion; one MacBook Pro laptop; one gray laptop cover; one semi-translucent, white cross-hatched zipbag containing childhood photos and photos of the day Maldon and her family arrived in the United States; one Tommy Hilfiger backpack made from 100 percent polyester; one silk drawstring bag containing one brown Rado watch and one pair of glasses with red-and-black rims; two Pilot G2Premium

.38mm retractable pens; one Agha Shahid Ali poetry collection, *The Country Without A Post Office*, which was the color of her Rado watch; one book with the title *Sheep Machine;* and one Three Ladies spring roll rice paper wrappers.

EARTH: Oh my.

MALDON: My entire life.

EARTH: How efficient you are.

Eight days into her period, the poet in Normandy told her to consume chaste berry. For reasons beyond her intuitive comprehension, Maldon found herself beside herself, feeling out of her skin, disturbed. She continued to bleed, though not heavily. Perhaps due to the tumultuous nature of her mental circumstance, her body was unable to find equilibrium within its disrupted female ecosystem. She climbed into bed to breathe. Not long afterward, a headache bloomed like a thunderstorm inside her mind. Palpitations drummed in agitation against her chest. Time seemed to slow down by speeding up the environ of her body. She got under the covers to shut out the world, but the afternoon light reflected brightly, vibrantly commanding the center of her attention. She found it impossible to hide in broad daylight. Her eyelids were acute, fierce, and earsplittingly awake. How can I outrun my own reality? Maldon asked herself rhetorically. Then she remembered Planet Earth the night before. How she sat in her chair to breathe, to exist, when she could have crawled into her New Jersey bed. She could hear Planet Earth's breath undulating, surrendering itself to time and its anachronistic impulses. The night inside her was lucid and clear. Her lover, a botany of absolute profound stillness, sat in a chair while the physiology and ecology of her existence ceased its geological period to become one with Maldon's own grammar of existence. Over there, a plant was a pronoun. The moonlight falling on the rocking chair was an alphabet of feminine intellectual solitude. And the nouns were the adverbs sitting alone on a plate of grapefruits and blackberries. The conjunctions were holding each other's hands because the adverbs were squatting in a dilapidated building made of phonetics and clauses and orthographical prepositions. Maybe language was a generic technique for death, but she welcomed its phonetic law of syntax, her lover's breath giving way to anthropological placidity. When she sat in her chair, Maldon wondered if her lover was kindly, equably, and even-temperedly saying goodbye to her. And so the following morning when Planet Earth did not text her back, she came to believe the insouciant, unpredictable departure of it all and considered that this even-tempered adieu may as well be a bon voyage for the both of them.

It was not impossible for her to love this. She did not want her lover to leave for harbor. How could she forsake the deep howling wind that sat at the bottom of her heart? When her mother drove her to the supermarket to buy three bags of green beans and one Bosc pear, she educated Maldon on the art of roaring clamor.

MOTHER: You must make your lovers feel terrified about losing you.
MALDON: Why, Mother?
MOTHER: Fear keeps the seeds of their desire for you alive.
MALDON: Who cares.

MOTHER: A wolf can't just eat grass and expect to have voracious teeth.

MALDON: But a cow can.

MOTHER: Are you a cow?

MALDON: Fear keeps everyone pregnant while preparing for miscarriages.

MOTHER: I am not pregnant.

MALDON: But you are pregnant with fear.

MOTHER: I'm not afraid.

MALDON: You're afraid he would abandon you and go after some young sylph.

MOTHER: The fear is not there.

Then Maldon remembered. Not too long ago, in the early morning hours, Maldon had had a short conversation with God.

MALDON: It takes all of my mental strength to just exist.

GOD: I know.

MALDON: Permission to die, God.

GOD: No.

MALDON: Permission to not live forever.

GOD: No.

MALDON: Permission not to grow old without a soul mate.

GOD: No.

MALDON: Permission to experience instant amnesia.

GOD: Which is what death is, so NO.

MALDON: Permission to go to war with delusion.

GOD: No.

MALDON: The delusion that this life is worth living.

GOD: No.

MALDON: Permission to exercise obsolescence of self.

GOD: No.

MALDON: Permission to be excused from existence.

GOD: No.

MALDON: Permission to stop existing.

GOD: No.

MALDON: Permission to inhale poisons in all their deadly forms.

GOD: No.

MALDON: Gas.

GOD: No.

MALDON: Powder.

GOD: No.

MALDON: Liquid.

GOD: No.

MALDON: Permission to have the final say on when and how I die.

GOD: No.

MALDON: Permission to exit this dream called life.

GOD: Permissions denied. All of them.

MALDON: No no no no no!

GOD: Yes!

Before falling asleep, Maldon recalled, yes, Planet Earth had not departed and instead had told her that her brother had killed someone in her country and that he used wealth and his close relations with his cousin to flee the consequences of his crime, a crime that shamed her entire family. A few weeks before Christmas, Maldon's own father had kicked her out of his home. She hadn't spoken to him since. She had wanted to escape to the East

Coast to die, preferably Connecticut. Connecticut had leaning houses that looked like they could fall right into the sea. On quite a few occasions she had seen these slanted houses from the Amtrak window as the train took her deep into the New England anxiety of her travels. But now, other things seemed to occupy her mind: a mountain in Bavaria, a department store in Edinburgh. To make matters more consequential and elevated, the eighth planet from the Sun, Neptune, not the male deity of water and sea, had switched her mood stabilizer meds, meaning she had decided to get off and onto another kind of antidepressant. Her inner solar system went out of whack and decided to return to his hydrogenic and heliumic blueness. The entire planet had sobbed uncontrollably, and Maldon felt it was necessary for the sake of humanity's equatorial tranquility and all its ungodly eight satellites to travel to LA to help hug and calm the planet down. Right away, Maldon left her mother with her truck-driving fiancé and took the next Greyhound to the City of Angels. Immediately upon her arrival, Neptune, the planet, asked her where she wanted to eat and why she had lost so much weight.

NEPTUNE: Your face has shrunk.

MALDON: It's the poor angle at which you look at me.

NEPTUNE: No, impossible. Let me feed you. I know you love Fallopian food—I meant Ethiopian. We should have Ethiopian food!

MALDON: It's only twenty miles from here.

NEPTUNE: Let me plug that into my GPS.

MALDON: Actually, there is this Viet restaurant just 0.9 miles away. We should go there.

NEPTUNE: You sure? I know you love Ethiopian food.

MALDON: It's only 0.9 miles away. Not nearly the same distance.

NEPTUNE: What changed your mind?

MALDON: The word *blossom*. I love it.

The planet laughed at her addiction to the word "blossom." Neptune took her to a *phở* place with a lopsided, slightly elevated entrance. It was Blossom Los Angeles, near the border between homelessness (Skid Row) and Elysium (perverse heaven). Despite the planet feeling gassy, Maldon spent nearly twenty-four hours hugging it. During her short trip to LA, Maldon learned that Neptune had fallen in love with a film professor, and his attention had been on courting him. After bidding the planet Neptune farewell and an hour into her bus ride back into Su 890, the bus broke down with a flat tire. From her window, she watched bus passengers abandon the faulty bus and flee to an Arby's by the nearest gas station, Arco. However, unlike those fellow passengers, Maldon decided to stay on the bus. Then a U-turn sign miles away made her recall a conversation with Neptune about *cắt bao quy đầu*, cutting the foreskin of a three-year-old boy.

NEPTUNE: I thought your father was Catholic.

MALDON: Devotedly Catholic.

NEPTUNE: So why is he removing his son's foreskin?

MALDON: I don't know. He feels Islamic? Judaic?

NEPTUNE: Is he converting?

MALDON: No.

NEPTUNE: Your father is a funny one.

MALDON: What if all of your rings were forcefully removed from you?

NEPTUNE: It wouldn't hurt?

MALDON: What if your moons—Despina, Thalassa, and Naiad—stop orbiting?

NEPTUNE: Because my atmospheric foreskin has been circumcised by the universe?

MALDON: Yeah.

NEPTUNE: And my three moons have nothing to orbit?

MALDON: Exactly.

NEPTUNE: I would cry and maybe be more gaseous?

An hour and a half later, a bus arrived from Anaheim to switch the fifty-two restless, heavily snack-fed passengers from one lopsided bus to the other. The transfer was quick and efficient. Fifteen miles later, the insouciant driver announced that she had neglected to do a head count. In a tone of casual irony, she promised the passengers that at the Riverside stop, she would do the most useless honorable thing: she would count heads, which provoked a roar of laughter from the crowd, though what would happen to the voluptuously carnal passengers of the bus had she said instead that she would be giving head? Sitting on the second deck of the bus, Maldon had access to a comprehensive view of the city passing behind her and those diminutive compact cars, which were weaving in and out of the body of the long freeway. Life from this panoramic altitude appeared sonorous and metrological. At the Riverside stop, she noticed the yellow logo for Megabus on the bus driver's shirt. The logo and its yellowness felt pedophilic to her, but what fashion police could ever stop her from feeling this way about a bus sign? Could the cultural figure and critic Chris Kraus alter her perception of Megabus? And did the planet Neptune inform her that the world needed someone who was willing to fuck an alternative version of Kathy Acker for the sake of cultural posterity? She wanted to say farewell to a concubine, but she didn't really have a concubine to say goodbye to. Not really. There were some bad people below her who were transporting heroin and cocaine into the city, opium-ing the world with analgesic poppy, providing the city a false, calculated sense of addictive apathy. Meanwhile, Maldon's mother was marinating lamb chops with rosemary, black pepper, thyme, and some Maldon (salt) in olive oil and butter. The way her mother said "rosemary," so conspicuously sharp and drawn out, it made Maldon think immediately of rosemary being a person as opposed to being an herb, as if Maldon's mother was trying to convince rosemary to bathe with uncooked lamb, as if it would be a balmy experience for its shrubby evergreen soul.

MOTHER: Why is lamb meat so stinky?

MALDON: What do you mean stinky?

MOTHER: It's especially stinky around the fat.

MALDON: You did soak the young fatty sheep in lots of herbs.

MOTHER: It still hasn't fended off its wild, brutish odor.

MALDON: Beef is much more tender.

MOTHER: Well, if you dig into its center it's quite juicy and delicate.

MALDON: I'd rather clothe my tongue—

MOTHER: In what?

MALDON: A full-bodied vintage white.

MOTHER: You know we don't drink wine.

MALDON: Besides, sheep like to sleep in red.

MOTHER: I don't trust anyone who rinses his mouth.
MALDON: With alcohol.
MOTHER: You know. You know.

By the time she climbed into bed, the planet Neptune had asked if an asteroid had walked by her and if there were any leaves rustling like stars between her thighs. Not too long ago, she recalled, yes. She did not want to be like the Chinese poet Hai Zi, who committed suicide by taking a nap on the railroad tracks, nor charcoal-burnt Yoon Ki-won nor self-gunshotted Van Gogh nor Wally Wood nor Otto Weininger. Could Maldon starve herself like Amphicrates of Athens in order to get the job done? Did she have the unnecessary wisdom of Malik Bendjelloul or Robert W. Criswell to run in front of a train like Anna Karenina? How intolerant was she to hanging like film director Boris Barnet or actress Pratyusha Banerjee? Could she stab herself with a sword like Cato the Younger? What was the best way to die? In one's sleep? She did love poisoning very much: carbon monoxide poisoning, phenobarbital, barbiturate, alcohol, or paracetamol overdose. How about secobarbital pills? She did find herself not being too fond of starvation, nor wrist-slicing, nor self-immolation, nor self-strangulation, nor self-detonation with dynamite, nor drowning like Virginia Woolf, Alfonsina Storni, and Claude Jutra, nor self-cryogenic like Takako Konishi. What about suffocation via a grocery bag? What was Maldon fond of, exactly? Ritual seppuku disembowelment, jumping out of windows, hemlock poisoning, consumption of lye, and ingestion of weevil tablets were not her thing either. She was running out of lists of suicidal options. By the time she pulled a tree branch out of her body, she found that she didn't love potassium cyanide enough to want it to be a part of her exit plan. What exactly was she fond of?

She was fond of her mother not grieving over her dead body. But what about her dream of having a post-sarcophagus life? Must she abandon it altogether for now? Her mother had spent a score and a half years raising her, chiseling her into this female, human sculpture. Could she be so quick to vandalize it? To destroy years of massive construction on this thing called her being? She could cease to exist, yes, but what about her mother? Her mother who spent nearly fifty years lifting thirty boatloads of rocks from one island to the next so that they all would have a chance at floating out to sea. To create a new life under the young, weary heart of the Sun. Her mother who climbed thirty-seven mountains in her bare feet while trying to fight sea monsters and hydras, who endured severe dehydration and exhaustion, frostbites, lethal hellholes, crevasse falls, edema, instant dizziness, nightmare age, confusion, unforgivingly heavy snowfalls, tropical infections, whiteouts, collapsing of lungs and low oxygen, just so that she could survive one Himalaya to the next. To get her into college in Minnesota—yes, the state—demanded that Maldon's mother plant 17,000 acres of pine trees all over the state for the next eighteen years. Her mother had closed her eyes as if Minnesota was just a ghost, dug her heels in, and seeded the earth with these needle-shaped evergreen conifers until her fingers became straw and dust. Her mother had sacrificed her entire existence so that she could be where she was. She once told her mother how much she loved Uranus because it had twenty-seven natural satellites. Twenty-seven! Maldon had tried to befriend this gas giant, but all it did was orbit Neptune and Jupiter and blow icy gas at her. With an acute insight of her desire, her mother had even spoken to the planet Uranus on her behalf.

MOTHER: What will it take?

URANUS: For me to befriend your daughter?

MOTHER: Yes.

URANUS: I know I only orbit the Sun once every eighty-four—eighty-four!—years.

MOTHER: So?

URANUS: Parts of my axial self-experience about forty-two years of darkness.

MOTHER: So?

URANUS: Your suicidal daughter is already dark. You think after forty-two years of being exposed to no light, I want to be around such dark melancholia, sorrow, and dysthymia?

MOTHER: Even if, at times, her woe is mild?

URANUS: For being the iciest, wintriest planet in the solar system, I—

MOTHER: Her soul isn't a basin or a sinkhole, Uranus.

URANUS: Don't "Uranus" me.

MOTHER: What will it take?

URANUS: Tell me about your daughter.

MOTHER: She is made entirely of salt. I named her Maldon.

URANUS: I am icy. What would I need salt for? You are not trying to sell me remnants of Lot's wife, are you?

MOTHER: No, no, of course not. I would never try to sell ice to Inuit.

URANUS: Why did you name her Maldon?

MOTHER: When she was in my womb, I craved fish sauce. Terribly. I couldn't name her Squid or Ka-Me or Three Crabs or Red Boat Premium. Her friends would make fun of her.

URANUS: So you basically Westernized her existence so she could fit in.

MOTHER: Mr. Uranus, I crossed fifty-eight waterfalls, 861 rivers, and sifted through millions of acres of forest trees just so my daughter wouldn't need to suffer. If I Westernized her a little, it doesn't mean I don't love her.

URANUS: I see.

MOTHER: So?

URANUS: So, around February-something I hang out near the constellation Pisces the Fishes. Tell her I will make my ghostly visit there, and we can hang out for a little bit.

MOTHER: Instead of offering Buddha seven bananas, three persimmons, a handful of grapes, two cherimoyas, and apple custards like I usually do, this Saturday I will offer them to you, Mr. Uranus.

URANUS: I am not a god, you know.

MOTHER: If one is cold, which you are, befriending them is a godlike feat.

URANUS: You do know that during the allegorical Golden Age, my son Kronos dethroned me, right?

MOTHER: Your son has balls.

URANUS: More of them now that he has castrated me.

MOTHER: How did he manage that?

URANUS: He destroyed me with a sickle.

VI KHI NAO

MOTHER: That's sick!
URANUS: And then he threw my testicles into the mouth
          of Poseidon.
MOTHER: Is Poseidon gay?
URANUS: If he wasn't before, he is now.
MOTHER: Whose idea was it to castrate you?
URANUS: My other son's.
MOTHER: Some sons . . . One good thing did come out of
          that callousness.
URANUS: What is that?
MOTHER: Your severed testicle did produce a beautiful,
          frothy thing.
URANUS: It did, didn't it?
MOTHER: Aphrodite.
URANUS: Well, my foamy daughter instigated the Trojan
          War . . . .
MOTHER: Let's not mention it.
URANUS: I can't help being dark. . . .
MOTHER: You will get along fine with my daughter.

Maldon thought, after all of her mother's metaphysical efforts,
the least she could do for her was to purely exist. Yet every
day she woke up bearing chthonic cravings, welcoming death
as if it were breakfast: pancakes not so flat. In the middle of
the night, Maldon woke up with a heaviness, like lead, on her
chest. The planet Neptune had decided that it would fly to
Cloud to be with Maldon to nurse her back into existence.
Planet Neptune had reserved an Airbnb in Alpha Tau that was
obscenely overpriced. The entire house cost nearly 2K for only
about two weeks' worth of convalescence.

MALDON: 2K? Really, Neptune?

NEPTUNE: I searched, alright. Searched and searched.

MALDON: Impossible.

NEPTUNE: This was the best option. Available for our dates and close to the hospital.

MALDON: My god.

NEPTUNE: It's my gift to you, Salt.

MALDON: No!

NEPTUNE: Take it as a gift and chill.

MALDON: 2K for two weeks?

NEPTUNE: It's a whole house!

MALDON: We could book a bedroom or two before the surgery.

NEPTUNE: Right. I've planned with the surgery in mind. We can't be sharing a place with anyone as you will be recovering.

MALDON: A hotel for two weeks would be cheaper.

NEPTUNE: Salt, we have no idea when exactly the surgery is happening. I didn't want to book last minute.

MALDON: You could have asked Pluto to help you.

NEPTUNE: Pluto doesn't know shit, and it's no longer a planet. It's dwarfed, remember?

MALDON: Oh, god.

NEPTUNE: Look, Salt. I don't want to go around jumping from place to place. Too tiring for me. It's easier to stick with this plan than to change it now.

MALDON: I see.

NEPTUNE: Have you packed yet?

MALDON: No.

NEPTUNE: Don't worry about it. It's a gift.

Maldon felt morbidly aggrieved and didn't know whom to express this depth of debt and despair to. Planet Neptune kept assuring Maldon that this was a gift from her inner wealthy solar core, and despite having no natural satellite and no atmosphere, its email-like quicksilver heart had the ability to help Maldon recover rapidly and eloquently from heart surgery and potentially syphilis, too, if Maldon felt compelled to acquire this kind of bacterial-disease-inducing sexual intercourse just for the sake of added cardiovascular challenge. Though Maldon did wonder how effective Neptune would be at decreasing the impairment to her central nervous system if she did, by chance or impulse, allow syphilis to visit her body for a week or two. The planet Neptune had loved her a great deal, yet Maldon did not feel that what she was giving her was a gift when the cost of her convalescence depressed the lever of both fiscal debt and noneconomical obligation on Maldon's soul. She felt its non-monetary sovereign weight, its potential, unspoken repayments in principal and interest. What kinds of emotional bonds, mortgages, notes, loans, and psychological obligations would this indebtedness accrue for her? The enormity of the heft and liability burdened her, and freights of panic began to unravel their misery through her subliminally waking state. She felt the weight of regret pressing on her. She regretted allowing the planet to help her, to fly with her to Cloud, to book the Airbnb on her behalf. And, as if inconspicuously, though she had not intentionally provoked or stroked that small, insignificant ember into a desolate beast, she felt the wild fire of that debt unraveling uncontrollably out of her. Maldon did wonder if this was the universe's ontological way of holding her prisoner, of preventing her from orbiting out of life; if her soul felt the weight of obligation and connection, when the analgesia gently put her body to sleep, her mind and soul, aggravated by debt, would not be able to fall into that soporific trap. The ontological immune system of the human soul used emotional, fiscal, psychological, and spiritual debts to combat the disease of nihilism and the infirmity of suicide. This was one way human existence exerted a psychological check and balance on itself. The human species is a self-preserving organism. Even if Maldon felt the intolerable impulse to commit suicide, other protective systems of being, other social and agricultural and fiscal immune systems would self-activate themselves through convoluted associations and connections so that Maldon could not resolve her binds by simply dying. Her desire to die would have to outcompete the impenetrable mainframe of debt. So, how had others done it? Bypassed this impenetrable mainframe and completed their suicidal mission? How did others empty their souls of obligations so that they could orbit out of existence? The planet Neptune had once told her, "Please, let me be the reason why you are existing." Though Maldon hadn't responded to that highly suggestive invitation, its pure presence and verbal actuality had drilled a profound linchpin into her thoughts so that she could not simply ignore it by ignoring. And, then, Maldon had an epiphany. One could never end debt. Debt was a part of life in one form or another, and if she was ready to commit suicide, she would just need to close her eyes and jump. It was that simple. Or not quite.

Rice cooked the night before consistently tastes better. In the morning Maldon and her mother ate sautéed chicken with white rice cooked the day before, before heading to the storage facility to collect the ten-foot U-Haul to transport her stuff from her mother's friend's garage. Their stomachs were filled with rice, and monsoon before the feet of the buffaloes trampled on them. At her friend's garage, Maldon watched her mother lift boxes and containers into the truck. She could smell the sweat and labor off the skin and backs of the men her mother had hired.

MALDON: Mother, you hired these men to work for you. Why are you lifting?

MOTHER: They charge per hour.

MALDON: Let them carry these for you.

MOTHER: Shut up, Salt.

MALDON: I think you ought to rest a little.

MOTHER: If I am not there to push them along, they are going to take all day. And they wouldn't know how to stack things.

MALDON: They have done this for seven years. Surely, they must know how domestic Tetris works.

What her heart condition has taught her: how to let others manifest her dreams for her. To let go of control. To let others carry the burden for her. She didn't need to do everything. Even if she wanted to help her mother, she couldn't. She couldn't lift without dying, without placing enormous strain on her heart and smearing it with the weight of its counter resistance. She wanted her mother to experience this new freedom. This freedom of being submissive to men and their sense of time. So what if they charged per hour? Let them. There was so much beauty in watching others work for her objects. Her belongings. There was so much beauty in doing nothing. So much beauty in the act of visual consumption, which was what observing entailed. Maldon wanted her mother to enjoy this. To love this. To embrace this non-laborious life. But her mother climbed into the truck and dove into the labor. Lifting. Bending. Shifting. Grabbing. Demanding to be the director of these two men in a film called *Storage Space*, about an interspatial dimension with boxes of fabric and units of endless absence. Of light. Of human contact and touch. All of this spatial noise was making Maldon dizzy. She wanted to sleep a little, to faint a little in front of these muscular men. After she grew tired of watching them sweat, she turned to one of the cacti in her mother's friend's driveway and studied its acidity. It was succulently short and spiny.

MALDON: How are you today?
CACTUS: Dry.
MALDON: Would you like some of my water?
CACTUS: No.
MALDON: Be that way then.

Three weeks ago, she had been so excited to die. The infection had attacked her heart the morning of her teaching, and she was excited that the primary engine of her existence had had the fortunate opportunity to break down (completely, she was so hopeful) so that she could die. Immediately. She was sad to see that she was breathing again. Her heart refused to be donated to Goodwill; who would want to second-handedly buy a broken machine? But why did her mother eat so healthy? Exercising and doing boring yoga, eating green beans and cabbage and edamame and cleansing her system with fresh apples. Drinking six glasses of water a day. At the healthy rate at which she was existing, Maldon was disappointed to know that her mother might live forever. How could she ever pen her suicide instead of penciling it in? Every year she would need to erase the calendar of her suicide and begin from scratch. As an inventor, Maldon tried to send out as many patents as possible. In case she did die, her mother would have the money from her inventions to live on in her retirement.

Then the planets Saturn and Venus texted her.

SATURN: Dear Salt, I'm already old and set in my ways. Yet you are the catalyst for such new, pleasant, and surprising unfoldings in me. Radical vulnerability.

VENUS: Good morning, Salt. I've made you a cup of your favorite tea with dahlia and fruit and a branch of magnolia fresh from the garden.

When the planet Saturn returned home that evening, she spoke on the phone with Maldon. Maldon relayed to her the event of her near-death experience not too long ago.

MALDON: You know, that day I packed for death.

SATURN: You stunned us.

MALDON: I stoned?

SATURN: No, you stunned Planet Earth and me.

MALDON: What do you mean?

SATURN: I remember looking at you and thinking, what the hell?

MALDON: I see.

SATURN: No one comes into my office and casually says that they almost died. You were so casual about it.

MALDON: As one is.

SATURN: That was a lesson.

MALDON: In what?

SATURN: In Maldonness.

MALDON: I see.

SATURN: What if you had died that day, Salt?

MALDON: You would have known my mother.

SATURN: I told you about that woman who died.

MALDON: Yes, you did.

SATURN: They didn't find her until a week later.

MALDON: Yes.

SATURN: Her family was so sad.

MALDON: I can imagine.

The following morning Maldon flew into Alpha Tau and left her mother in Su 890.

When she first entered it, the Airbnb house smelled like   manure—the unadorned feces of several feral cows—but it gave her a sense of borrowed freedom, one that was temporarily lent to her for a night. She had shared houses, beds, and rooms with others in the last six years or so, and it was nice to have something of her own. Even though Planet Neptune had kindly booked it as a gift for her. By evening, her stomach was growling from waiting too long to eat. The glass-top electric stove took too long to fire up, and it forced her to warm the recently cooked rice and chicken in the oven. To curb her hunger, she threw some nuts and dark chocolate into her mouth, but her metabolism may have been obscenely too effective. Five minutes later she was starving again. If she ate, she would have to wait until her body digested the food before sleeping. Between two conflicting impulses, the desire to sleep and the desire to eat, she preferred the former to the latter, and she told herself, fuck this, I don't need to eat. By the time she spoke on the phone with Planet Earth, Planet Earth had already fallen asleep. She could hear the Earth snoring remotely and ambiently through the cellphone, like listening to the static noise of a radio as it announced the days leading up to World War II. Unjustifiably, there was something enigmatic and comforting about listening to the Earth grunting energetically and consistently. Maldon could feel the vibration of the Earth's equatorial diameter. The Earth was about 4,600 million years old. So, if it grunted a little during sleep, Maldon felt like she could understand.

Earlier, when she had placed the chicken into the skillet and turned on the stove, she recalled, yes, the Uuber driver was very kind to wait for her outside Price Chopper so she could buy one head of cabbage, a whole pre-smoked and pre-baked chicken, five pounds of enriched white rice, some green onions, one box of mixed nuts, and one large pre-baked apple pie. The Uuber driver apologized for how long it took her to collect her from the airport. Maldon had waited about twenty minutes, which was unusually long. But Maldon didn't mind it. She enjoyed watching people getting in and out of shuttles, being collected by family members (yes, such familiar chivalry still existed), and studying the footsteps of passersby. The way they fell onto the ground. She found the steps mesmerizing. Observing mundane gestures slowed down her mind and retarded her emotions so that she could not be too quick to adjust her consciousness to a new place.

The Airbnb looked like a modern bungalow from the 1800s. The siding was painted a light blue, a blue that was darker than the color of the sea. There was a white deck attached to the house. There was a small stair leading to the main entrance of the house. The first thing Maldon did when she entered the over-priced Airbnb was to use the toilet. She lifted the immaculate seat, turned around, pulled down her pants, and, while she urinated, she thought that the white towel in front of her face looked like an angel's scrotum. Should she dry her hands after washing them with aloe vera soap? When she pulled several tissues from the bathroom's Kleenex box, she thought to herself: it's not an angel's scrotal cloth; it smells distinctively bovine and pastoral. Should I continue wiping my face with it? One cherubic testicle for God. One for me. One for God. When she pulled the toilet paper to wipe her clit, she formed no opinion about its pristineness. By the time she exited the bathroom, her brother had texted her.

BROTHER: Have you arrived?

MALDON: Yes.

BROTHER: Weren't you supposed to text us when you arrived?

MALDON: Yes, I am sorry brother. I should have been less thoughtless.

BROTHER: By any chance, do you have any photos of us when we first arrived in America?

MALDON: Why?

BROTHER: I only have one photo where I was smiling.

MALDON: That one? Why weren't you smiling in your other childhood photos?

BROTHER: I knew quite young that I had a flat nose and was Asian, and if I smiled, my smile would flatten my nose even more.

MALDON: That's a terrible reason to stop smiling.

BROTHER: At any rate, I went to the dentist, and they deep cleaned my teeth and removed one tooth. The doctor thinks I have brittle bone. It's genetic. He wanted to see my childhood teeth.

MALDON: One childhood photo of you smiling can determine your bone DNA?

BROTHER: Yeah. Can you look for it?

MALDON: It's in Su 890.

BROTHER: Do you know where it is?

MALDON: I know where.

BROTHER: If it's not too much to ask.

MALDON: I can ask Mom to take a photo of it for you.

BROTHER: I don't want her to go through your things. Not everyone likes it.

MALDON: I know where it is.

When she woke up the following day, she was in a terrible mood. Her wild, windy indignation stretched quite beastly across her chest and precipitously uprooted her. Standing in front of the long door-length window of the Airbnb, she noticed a white grocery bag being tossed and pushed around in the wind as it tried to move closer to a neighbor's garage, and she thought of the film *American Beauty*. How she loved the ending. Kevin Spacey's falling face as his head leaked blood. Had she returned to Cloud to die after all? thought Maldon. Would her desire to fall off the Earth completely defy the law of conservation? Did she view life so terribly that she would not ever want to return or revisit? What were the chances of the Airbnb coming with eleven chickens? It worked out because Planet

Neptune was a Muslim, and Islamic planets had a tendency to abstain from consuming pork. The only alternate white meat was these somatic chickens.

By flying red-eye, Planet Neptune arrived in the early hours, at the same time that Maldon's rage was opening like a wildflower. Planet Neptune was struggling to lift a piece of blue luggage that was twice its equatorial diameter (about thirty-thousand miles) up the small stairs of the house's deck. Maldon would have liked to help Neptune lift, but since Planet Neptune was ambivalent about her or his gender and didn't want Maldon to injure her heart, Maldon had no choice but to stand near the long sofa and watch this remote gas giant suffer.

NEPTUNE: There are so many chickens here!

MALDON: You should see them roost and crow in the early morning hours.

NEPTUNE: It's so dark and dreary outside!

MALDON: Let me ask one of the eggs if they would let you eat them.

NEPTUNE: Don't bother forcing an abortion out of her. I'm not hungry.

MALDON: Fine. How is Triton?

NEPTUNE: Still photomosaically happy.

MALDON: What does that mean?

NEPTUNE: I think it means that it's hydrostatically balanced and not hysterical.

MALDON: What does that mean, though?

NEPTUNE: I have no idea. All I know is that its rotation is tidally locked to my heart.

MALDON: What does that mean?

NEPTUNE: Abort that child for me, will you?
MALDON: Right away. Sunny-side up?
NEPTUNE: No, no, no. Neptune-side up.

Planet Neptune ate the egg with half his eye closed and half
of her other eye open. His sexuality was half in transit between a him and a her, and if Maldon was so willing, it could
easily transition into an it or them. It made Maldon think of
the "it" in the term *bánh ít trần* and then reminded her of *thêm*,
which, translated into Vietnamese, meant additional or more
or extra as in extra sex, which was what that word actually
meant, in context or out of context, for the object of a verb or
preposition to denote two or more persons or items previously
cited. Please, *thêm*. Please *ít*. To imply less. Please *ít*. He ate the
egg quietly and studiously without transitioning to *thêm* salt or
pepper.

Miscommunication between Neptune and Maldon led to confusion as to the time of Maldon's appointment with Dr. Cephei.
The following morning Maldon woke up early to call Alpha
UMi Aa Hospital to confirm. She discovered it was later in the
afternoon but found that she could not fall back to sleep. Time
seemed to betray her, traveling far and wide into a future that
did not belong to anyone, especially not to Maldon. A sense of
anachronistic hopelessness invaded Maldon's soul. Planet Neptune, who had chosen to arrive in Cloud to nurse Maldon back
to health before and after surgery, was also a PhD candidate
at Agastya Institute in Southern California and had a massive
paper of thirty or so pages to write for his final. Maldon passed
her long, sleepless days pretending to be Ganymede, Jupiter's
largest moon. Some moons were bigger than planets or former

planets, such as Neptune and Pluto. Ganymede, discovered by Galileo in 1610, had such a spherical dilemma. Ganymede was the only moon that had its own magnetic meadow. Maldon also felt compelled to be Ganymede because supposedly it kept a secret, subterranean ocean inside its deep groovy or sulcus-y heart. Who wouldn't want that?

The hospital was a semi-colossal cement brick housing four major windows. The windows looked like the ones from the twelve extraterrestrial spacecraft from the Denis Villeneuve science fiction film *Arrival*, with Amy Adams starring so brilliantly as an extraterrestrial translator. Maldon and Neptune took the elevator up to the sixth floor. They had expected to see a heptapod making annular, linguistic shapes with its futuristic tentacles, but instead they were greeted by a receptionist named Bell Pepper who moved slowly, like a doorknob. Her slowness made Maldon laugh, but Neptune was infuriated. A few alabaster octogenarians and septuagenarians also moved as slowly as Bell Pepper to fill out paperwork. Young Maldon felt completely out of place, and it didn't help her that she had developed a linear perception of her life: one in which she wanted a definitive cul-de-sac with breath. Not too soon after, they met Dr. Cephei, who, not surprisingly, looked heptapodic. He shook their hands and informed them that minimally invasive surgeries were duplicitous. Most surgeries, especially cardiovascular surgeries, were always invasive. A perfusionist would oversee the cardiopulmonary bypass machine, which basically meant that the blood from Maldon's heart and lungs would need to travel out of her body the distance of a tennis court so that her heart could be made still and isolated from the drama of oxygen and other physiological phenomena, and the surgeon could operate on her heart alone. Such tennis-sized exposure of her vitals was, by definition, anything but non-invasive. Before falling asleep after Uubering back to their Airbnb, Maldon received a call from the planet Saturn, who wanted to know how her hospital appointment had unfolded.

SATURN: That is terrible.

MALDON: And the wait list is terrible.

SATURN: Your life quality and expectancy would go down massively.

MALDON: It excites me that I won't live forever.

SATURN: How long would the new heart last?

MALDON: Five to ten years.

SATURN: That's terrible.

MALDON: The new mechanical valve, however, lasts an eternity and looked like a clitoris inside of a circle the size of a quarter.

SATURN: Really? An eternal mechanical clit.

MALDON: With swinging metal doors.

SATURN: Like those wooden saloon doors in Western films?

MALDON: Yeah. Leaflets.

SATURN: Would I hear a gun battle between you and God if I stood outside that door?

MALDON: You would hear a mechanical click.

SATURN: Would that mean you're going to die?

MALDON: It just means that the valve is working. But the cardiovascular team is going to stop my heart for the valve replacement operation.

SATURN: So, you are going to die a little.

MALDON: Just for three or so hours.

SATURN: That should make you happy, being able to casually extinguish that way.

MALDON: I find no happiness in that.

SATURN: Because it's temporary?

MALDON: I suppose you can say that.

SATURN: I suppose. I suppose. Did the surgeon say anything about complications?

MALDON: With the mechanical valve?

SATURN: Yeah.

MALDON: The leaflets could get stuck.

SATURN: Then you would have the opposite problem.

MALDON: Yes. Instead of my heart leaking or regurgitating, stenosis develops.

SATURN: Oh, to survive in this galaxy.

MALDON: Or not.

SATURN: When is your surgery?

MALDON: I need more tests first. At a different hospital.

SATURN: How come?

MALDON: It's a small hospital and doesn't have that kind of man power.

SATURN: Humans.

Planet Neptune woke up from his nap and waddled around the Airbnb like a hyper-self-conscious, giggling duck. Meanwhile, Maldon was boiling fat rice noodles, stirring and frying cabbage with green onions, and baking beef with seven Yukon potatoes sliced in halves. The kitchen was highly active with heat and commotion as the ants, to express their multifarious, manic industry with restlessness, marched in and out of cabinets in search of sugar and honey. Maldon wanted the planet to complain to the Airbnb host about this complex communal colony, but Neptune was smiling brightly in her post-soporific bliss.

NEPTUNE: Maldon, Maldon.

MALDON: What is it, Nep? What is it?

NEPTUNE: I had this super weird dream about urinating.

MALDON: Frozen nitrogen?

NEPTUNE: No, urine. I was urinating so much that I flooded the bathroom, and I peed so much that it all turned into poop. Can you believe that?

MALDON: Why were you peeing so much?

NEPTUNE: Maybe because I am the densest and I am seventeen times the mass of the Earth? And, with global warming, my ice is melting?

MALDON: I think climate change only impacts Earth's ecosystem.

NEPTUNE: You mean it doesn't extend intergalactically?

MALDON: No, not really.

NEPTUNE: For parts of me being so cryovolcanic, to borrow my beloved Triton's retrograded words, why am I urinating so much?

MALDON: Well, only in your dreams, gas giant.

NEPTUNE: But still.

The Airbnb grew annoying for both the blue planet and Maldon. Every five minutes, the earsplitting heater kept vomiting this raucous, blooming noise that could split Maldon's veins open. Each time the heater regurgitated in its throat with cacophonous hot air, she cowered and covered her ears with her hands to prevent them from disturbing the serene content of her inner hemostasis. Maldon knew that leasing this exorbitant Airbnb had been a bad idea, but the emotional economy of inertia persuaded them both to lodge and remain. She regretted not sojourning to other housing possibilities. Every now and then, Maldon would suggest that they relocate to Cloud City, where there was more culture and less isolation. But with his heart bent on this Airbnb, the planet Neptune convinced Maldon otherwise. We only have two weeks here, Nep said. And then we can move. I hate shuffling around like a deck of cards, he re-emphasized. When they walked to an ice cream shop to grab an ice cream shake and a butterscotch cone, Maldon suggested to Nep that they should start making formal complaints to the host about the rogue ants, the fortissimo radiator, the surfeit of chickens squawking in the early morning hours of their awakening, and how it took three hours to get the stove to heat up. For most of the day, Neptune was in a terrible mood. The walk to the ice cream parlor made it worse. The wind, though fresh and refreshing at first, began to annex his earlobes and bald, blue skull with severe air. By throwing her arms in front of his face, Neptune was able to dodge some of it, but it was still too much. Maldon, who was used to this brutal climate, came to the walk with more preparation. She had donned a thick wool hat, and her Russian sheepskin coat with a stand-up collar made of genuine astrakhan fur kept her from feeling the abrasive bullwhip of the wind. Even so, the Earth's ecosystem was shattering them, and they had no choice but to walk quickly home.

NEPTUNE: Do you know we have a backyard?
MALDON: Oh, really?

NEPTUNE: I walked in it a bit earlier.
MALDON: How was it?
NEPTUNE: There was no deck. No chair.
MALDON: A travesty.
NEPTUNE: A dead backyard with no life.
MALDON: Let's make a formal complaint. Get our refund
           and then book another place.
NEPTUNE: No.

At home, the radiator reinitiated its hot-air purging ritual. Maldon stood near the door-length window and studied the leaves in their near post-mulching state, rolling and twirling heavily in the wind. The timeless weight of the air's melancholia and late spring misery created a basin of forlornness in the Earth's residual fauna of weather unfolding and folding. There was morbid darkness and murkiness. The house, surrounded by the weight of restfulness and the weight of soundlessness, sat like a tub of vanilla ice cream waiting for the Sun to melt it all away. Standing in front of the mirror of time and watching the Sun descend into the armpit of the night, Maldon recalled a conversation she had had earlier with her former lover, Earth.

EARTH: I'm awake.
MALDON: How was work?
EARTH: Quiet. I got a lot done.
MALDON: Excellent.
EARTH: How are you feeling today?
MALDON: I am a little angry at the planet Neptune.
EARTH: Why?
MALDON: It has always been a struggle between us. I

appreciate that she came all the way from Southern California to care for me.

EARTH: What is the struggle this time? It's been three days. And I believe he slept all of the first day.

MALDON: I guess the same reason I broke up with Neptune.

EARTH: Is this just a personality clash, or is there an issue or several issues?

MALDON: It's a personality clash. He is really sweet and kind to me.

EARTH: I'm sorry to hear this. You need peace and caring right now.

MALDON: I worry she can't offer that.

EARTH: This is difficult, Maldon. I thought you were going to be well cared for and have some peace.

MALDON: I knew this ahead of time. It was my fault.

EARTH: It's not your fault. You need his help with doctors and appointments.

MALDON: Yes.

EARTH: Is there another procedure that you would prefer?

MALDON: Ideally no valve replacement at all.

EARTH: That's not possible because of the deterioration. If you don't have it, you'll need a heart transplant, which means death.

MALDON: I know, Planet Earth. I know.

EARTH: I'm sorry, Salt. I know you want to die.

MALDON: I really do. I really do.

EARTH: I have to admit that I can understand Neptune's side in not letting you kill yourself, Salt.

MALDON: I understand his side too.

EARTH: I just want to swim in your ocean.

MALDON: Why, Earth?

EARTH: Because, Salt.

Because dear, Salt.

I want to live in your ocean. Is it raining with you?

MALDON: Perhaps it is always raining inside me.

EARTH: Are you too sad, Salt?

MALDON: I am not sad, Earth. There is a difference here.

EARTH: Yes?

MALDON: Not wanting to live doesn't equal depression.

EARTH: You plan to prove this theory how? I'm going to need more convincing.

MALDON: When you eat a good ice cream and you are full, do you want to force-feed yourself another liter?

EARTH: No, I don't.

MALDON: I feel the same way about life.

Maldon couldn't quite get it. How had a simple walk to the ice cream parlor generated so much tension between her and the planet Neptune? The strain was sharp, and there was much hostility in the Cloud air. The antagonism of doing things for others and on behalf of others. It filled both their chests with rage and ill feeling. Neptune tried to pay for the ice creams with the credit card, but it was a cash-only venue. Frustrated, the planet tried to leave, but Maldon pulled him back in and pulled cash from both their pockets to pay. They had just seven dollars; they needed $7.28. The teenage receptionist waved the difference away. Yet Neptune insisted that this was a terrible place to be. Maldon couldn't understand. She would never understand. This well of isolation and misunderstanding between them. Their incompatibility. Their co-existence here. Their lack of free will. In between licking the butterscotch off the sugar cone, Maldon had thought, yes, the house made the planet suffocate. By evening, when Neptune closed the curtain the color of the mulched leaves outside, Maldon went introspective. Why didn't I die on the East Coast? Why didn't God give me permission? asked Maldon. She had packed quickly for death. Had sat on her Craigslist bed waiting for death to teleport her to the dimension of profuse darkness. But nothing had happened. Nada. Zilch. Zero. Nothing. Nay. Her heart returned to its regular rhythm, and life continued forth without her consent.

MALDON: This time I am not crying or weeping. I am as lucid as any species with a deep sense of awareness can be.

EARTH: Is that part of your struggle with Planet Neptune? She is a one-woman squad on a mission to save you?

MALDON: No. My mother is the armor that is preventing the bullet of death from entering me.

EARTH: I just want to hold you, Salt. I want to understand.

MALDON: You are holding me, Earth. You are.

Then, yes, Maldon recalled comforting the planet Neptune the day after his arrival in Cloud. He was crying because Maldon was trying to reason with her about death.

MALDON: I'm so tired of life. My mother is the only reason why I'm having this surgery.

NEPTUNE: Live for me.

MALDON: You are still so young. A young planet still. You are only 4.503 billion years old. Born from gas and dust. You will probably live another 4.6 billion years.

NEPTUNE: What does that mean?

MALDON: If I live for you, I would live forever. My mother is almost a dead star, a white dwarf.

NEPTUNE: And you want to swim with dead stars.

MALDON: I do, Nep. I do. Waiting for my mother and myself to be ousted as a planetary nebula.

NEPTUNE: I can't take this. I just can't.

Then the entire planet wept, tears falling at nearly 1,300 mph. It nearly blew out all of their Airbnb windows. It took five laundry baskets for Maldon to apprehend all of his tears. She had to continually feed the laundry baskets with blankets, bathroom towels, and comforters so they would soak up all of Neptune's melting lachrymal tributaries. When the planet finished crying, Maldon threw all of the overlays into the washer, dialed the machine to the highest spin mode to squeeze all the tears out, and tossed them into the dryer. Maldon did six loads before the Airbnb was desiccated again. This was a lesson for Maldon to keep her thoughts on death to herself. However, it did not escape Maldon that it was with some irony that her continued existence made it possible for her to capture these thoughts on the pages of this book. Re-examining Neptune's tear ducts, Maldon recalled, yes, that at the hospital, to borrow C.A. Conrad's titular words "while waiting in line for death," Neptune had narrated an unusual case she had read in her research.

NEPTUNE: A woman was rushed to the hospital with a severe case of blindness. The physicians didn't know what to do with her. Her eyes were sealed tight. With some inescapable, minor investigation, an ophthalmologist discovered that there were four un-dead, salt-sucking bees, tinier than buxom bumblebees, thriving under the twenty-nine-year-old's right eyelid, feeding off her tear ducts because they were probably on their periods and craving sweat, salt, cum.

Most bees feast on flowers. A lachrymal, cum-based diet—is that even possible? Maldon thought: Could I be one of those sweat-seeking, high-sodium-consumer bees? Should I be feasting on someone's scrotum? Clit? Do I crave salt and consume salt all the time? Perhaps I am such things? Before electrolytes could become edible light, before an apocalypse could manifest itself empirically, the imagination had to narrate itself in fiction, in eco-transparency, in logic, science, biology, and thoughts. While waiting in line for death, God kept pushing and throwing and letting people cut in front of her. People such as South Korean rapper Lee Hye-ryeon, chef Anthony Bourdain, designer Kate Spade, general Zhang Yang, writer Ernest Hemingway, gay pop star Leslie Cheung Kwok-wing, artist Vincent Van Gogh, photographer Diane Arbus, etc. Yes, yes, it was true that some of these folks committed suicide even before she was born so, anachronistically, she had not a lot of sympathy for God, but some. But God should never let contemporary, coeval people cut in front of her. After all, she had been standing in line for death for hours now, and her legs had gotten tired. She was ready to be unethical and assholic, but who would let her cut in line? Who?

Consumers and visitors of her past continued to (out of nowhere, it seemed, though they rarely came out of nowhere) message her on Facebook. There was one man from her bygone years, whom she had befriended when she was in graduate school. He was a Dominican janitor in the English department. She had loved him with a platonic plenitude only seen between immigrants who shared a depth of divergence, isolation, and polarity.

CERVANTES: Madonna Maldon, *hola vieja amiga.*
MALDON: Cervantes! *¿Qué pasa?*
CERVANTES: *Aquí viviendo el momento. ¿Y tu vida amorosa?*
MALDON: *Es difícil tener una vida amorosa cuando hay muchas vacas en* Cloud. . . .

To prevent the radiator from purging, Neptune shut the heat off so they could sleep uninterrupted. It was the best decision ever made between them. In the morning, in order to be warm, Maldon told the radiator that it could re-vomit again. The eleven chickens, though not decapitated by Horacio Quiroga, remained reticent like Anna Akhmatova. Silent mornings were the best kind of mornings for Maldon. In taciturnity, she found inner tranquility and respite.

Maldon spent her day reading. She read mostly male authors, which disappointed her greatly. She read H.G. Wells' *Time Machine, The Literary Conference* by César Aira, a biography of Samuel Beckett. Aira's book started out terribly, and when she told Neptune this, he felt that it was an attack on his soul since Aira was his favorite author. Most of the books she had with her were male written. She wanted to berate her consciousness for this oversight. She had an extraordinary excuse for an ordinary flaw: in Su 890, she had made it through most of the books written by female authors and had had no choice but to pack for Cloud these remaining books she had not read. It so happened that they were all male authors.

Before falling asleep Maldon read on the internet about a meteor shower. The following morning, Maldon was hoping to leap their bodies and heads forward so that she and Neptune could catch debris and small pieces of asteroidic materials, especially the magnificent tail end as the cometary burst approached the Sun. It had been five million years since Neptune had a decent shower, and, although Maldon showered regularly, she felt that since her brother, her sister, niece and nephew, and brother-in-law were all going to ride to a restaurant in one spaceship, it was important for them to have this anti-quiescent bath as it would metaphysically clean and scrub them of years of sullied solar grime. Maldon learned that the showerhead of a comet, such as Comet Hale-Bopp, was like a goliath pinwheel discharging icy materials as it bathed the spherical sky of their existence. Maldon felt the gravitational force of Neptune's resistance. He didn't really want to shower as she was still somnolent, lethargic, and groggy from being deep inside sleep's dense circular orbit. They had stayed up late watching three episodes of *Killing Eve* and they were both very tired. Especially Planet Neptune, because he'd gotten up a few hours before sunrise to have breakfast as her blue digestive system was growing. But Maldon persisted.

VI KHI NAO

MALDON: If it hadn't been five million years, I wouldn't
           ask you to.
NEPTUNE: Would you be mad at me if I don't?
MALDON: Everyone would be in one spaceship, and it's a
           tight space.
NEPTUNE: I want to catch the shower tonight, not this
           morning.
MALDON: By then it would be too late. I doubt that this
           comet's already elongated orbit would last that
           long.
NEPTUNE: Seriously, though, would you be mad if I just put
           on some clothes and perfume?
MALDON: It's not about madness. You have to understand
           this.
NEPTUNE: Fine. I'll catch the last tail end of it.
MALDON: Thank you. You'll probably catch the ion tail. . . .
NEPTUNE: I want the dust tail.
MALDON: Well, better hurry.

There was nothing elliptical or iridescent about her desire for
Neptune to catch this shower. She wanted her family to enjoy
Neptune's company as much as possible. It was hard for her to
relay this desire to the planet since Neptune was so sensitive.
Also, it was the first time the planet would meet her family. It
was an important event. While placing the planet's sensitivity
on the back burner of her mind, Maldon thought quickly of
the comet's hydrogen envelope. How at one point she wanted to
use it to send an epistolary missive to VY CMa, the profoundly
oxygen-rich, crimson, and fat hypergiant star whom Maldon
adored but could never get this superbly radiant beauty to fall

in love with her. Maldon has been warned about VY's latent paroxysm or potential for mushrooming. But this minor foible did not deter her from loving it exponentially and exceptionally. Perhaps she could write the letter without a hydrogen envelope. Who needed an envelope anyway in transporting a missive? Especially to a star at the tail end of its life? Dying had a way of making things arbitrary for Maldon. Anything could fuck itself off.

The best part of the mornings at the Airbnb for Maldon was the eleven chickens who wobbled out of their one-foot by one-foot by one-foot shadowboxes, one box per chicken, concaved into the walls of the house throughout. She called these eleven chickens her Gallus gallus football team. When they all moved in form, in their domesticated offensive positions, they made killer moves. Especially the wide receiver, Jerry Rice. Three shadowboxes were affixed to the living room, eight of them in the kitchen. In the morning the chickens mutely crowed from their shadowboxes, leaped from their open white cages, and squatted in the kitchen, where the hens dropped half a dozen eggs or so from their impeccable asses. In the evening, these domesticated fowls returned to their open cages like inmates from the Louisiana State Penitentiary, with their heads down and their opisthotic souls institutionalized by sleep and boredom. Sometimes Maldon felt moved by the matutinal heliotropic desire to have an edible sun in her mouth. She would crack these free-range, domesticated eggs into a frying pan for breakfast. Most of the time, though, she watched the gregarious eggs roll about before settling in an equilibrium of tranquility. Once in a while, while waiting for Planet Neptune to wake up, Maldon watched the neighborhood children bouncing a soccer ball on their wooden deck near a solo white plastic chair while the Sun sprawled out on the front lawn like a thin sweater. The soccer ball echoed with each bounce, and the incubated noise followed by the hollowed voice of the cement made Maldon think of a spy secretly listening in on a conversation through a nestful of hay. Inside the purse of time, a wallet of desire awaited her, but all Maldon wanted to do was throw this purse into a cosmic lake, where she would not be able to find it ever again. She stretched her legs on the sofa and studied her quarterback, her bewitching hen, hen Erin Rodgers born in Chico, California, who was wobbling around the living room like a sumo wrestler. Her feathery head was a tangled ribbon of red, refulgent light, and her wizened gullet was beguilingly weather-beaten.

MALDON: Why is your throat so gnarled?
QB: The constant snapping of the straps on my football helmet.
MALDON: I see.
QB: No, you don't see.
MALDON: Okay. I don't see then.
QB: Come, sit on my lap.
MALDON: No, you sit on my lap.
QB: Fine.

Maldon grabbed QB Erin Rodgers like she would have a small beer barrel and lifted her onto her thighs.

QB: Why are you so bony?
MALDON: I lost some weight.
QB: air enough.

MALDON: If I feed a chicken chicken (itself), then you
           would consider that chicken a cannibal, right?
           But what if you feed a carrot to a carrot?

QB: Are you asking me if a vegetable can ever be a
           cannibal?

MALDON: No. However, have you ever experienced the fol-
           lowing?

QB: Following what?

MALDON: Somnambular echo?

QB: No.

MALDON: Emotional echo?

QB: No.

MALDON: Autosexual echo?

QB: What is that?

MALDON: Never mind. Hysterical echo?

QB: No.

MALDON: Sensual echo?

QB: Absolutely not.

MALDON: Sensory echo?

QB: Huh?

MALDON: Whatever. Spectacular echo?

QB: Nope, I don't think so.

MALDON: Phallic echo? Or a carrot giving another carrot a
           back rub—

QB: What?

MALDON: Have you eaten a carrot before?

QB: I don't think I am a rabbit.

MALDON: Hyperassociative echo?

QB: No.

MALDON: Quack for me.

QB: Ducks quack, not chickens.

MALDON: If a chicken quacks, it's a sign of talent.

QB: Quack, quack.

MALDON: You are just a superior quarterback. You just are. Unconscious echo?

QB: What are you trying to get at?

MALDON: Symbolic echo?

QB: No. No.

MALDON: Spasmodic echo?

QB: Can we stop?

MALDON: Somatic echo? Unnameable echo? Psychotropic echo?

QB: I quit.

MALDON: What about phallic trauma?

QB: Never. I don't have that thing.

MALDON: Right.

QB: Slaughter me already.

MALDON: I'll get to it. What about this one last question?

QB: Shoot.

MALDON: Have you ever had a hypnotic echo where your fate experiences a modest twilight of some verbal trauma born on an economic phallus purchased by a biological merchant who hasn't endured irremediable moaning?

QB: WTF?

MALDON: I'm trying to prepare myself psychotically for your annihilation. And for me to know when I can emotionally slaughter you.

QB: What kind of quack psychoanalyst are you?

MALDON: I'm not.

The Airbnb had the worst sound insulation system in the world. No matter where Maldon went in the house, she could not escape the cacophony of noises combating each other near her unplugged, unfiltered eardrums. They followed her everywhere and drove her profanely mad. The ruckus of the dryer, the vomiting radiator, the planet Neptune flushing the toilet when he urinated, the refrigerator humming like a stupid grandfather, the coffee maker whistling like an incorrigible troublemaker, the wall clock with an unhandsome face that looked exactly like a constipated or bloated lily striking each second of its existence, the buzzing of the lawn mower in the far distance, the ringing sounds in her ears. Maldon tried to sit still and attempted to empty the columns of volumes from her consciousness through meditation, but each time she breathed it seemed as if she were blowing air into a balloon, the balloon being her sense of serenity, and all the breathing did was just make the size of the balloon bigger and bigger. Thus, meditation became an overinflated balloon waiting to pop. And, when it did pop, she threw Thích Nhất Hạnh in the air (the book she had been reading to calm herself) and bit her lips hard. The resilient, muted chickens each shut one of their eyes while trying to comb and scratch their wizened throats with each other's nails as they surrendered to Maldon's rage.

Each day the planet Neptune escorted the team, the gregarious football players, to urinate and defecate. They all followed Neptune out of the front door one by one, marching like indiscriminate ducks.

At eight a.m,, Maldon and Neptune took a space shuttle from their Airbnb to Enterprise. On the freeway they passed leafless trees still devoid of life from the brutal, arctic winter of the previous months. Their tall, skinny legs were soaked to the knees in the empty, sporadic Midwest swamps. Their hair and branches were fringed with electricity, and the empty, murky sky suspended like a dead, still half flag on spring's lagoon. They were taking this long road trip so that they could request the following tests to be done on Maldon's body: an echocardiogram, complete pulmonary function, a carotid duplex, and an angiogram. It was a hassle, but it would allow them to speed up the date of the operation. As they entered Interstate 1800 going east in their Nissan rental spaceship, Maldon recalled, yes, that she had been angry at the Airbnb in Westerlund. The host had written in the house's rules and regulations about the toilet seat, how it was imperative, a must for all guests, post-urination and post-defecation, to put the toilet seat down before flushing to prevent the overexcited bacteria from leaping off the highly gymnastic urine's and feces's back and inadvertently and thoughtfully contaminating the air and the toilet's bowl environs before being forced by gravity to yield in defeat, of course in defeat, by landing ubiquitously on the toilet bowl's rim like denotated, mephitic starlings after an apiary explosion. Maldon thought her directive was a bit anal but complied without much contretemps as she didn't want to make waves with her demented, temporary landlord—until she noticed that the host never put the toilet seat down after flushing. How hypocritical of her, thought Maldon, and gave herself permission to abandon the new ritual entirely. And now, months later, as the spaceship entered the freeway, the never-before-felt burst of anger about the two-faced ordeal discharged out of her like a bullet from a stored-away, unused gun. She was taken aback by the intensity of her anger, as if it had appeared out of nowhere to haunt her. Not soon after, she learned to accept it and even welcomed it. Anger and grief, and even happiness and jealousy, rarely arrive when they are supposed to, meaning linearly and sequentially and chronologically. They often arrive as non sequiturs and introduce themselves as the bastard, intolerable child that shouldn't have ever been born, let alone have the audacity to arrive at a thought's birthday party without an RSVP or a formal invitation. Maldon never hated surprises, but this was too much even for her.

As they passed through Mitchellville both the planets Venus and Jupiter texted her to let her know that the gothic Notre Dame was in flames. The stained glass was melting despite four-hundred firefighters dropping their lives left and right to hose down the fire. Paris was dying and would never be the same again. The roof had fallen through. The spires were gone. Everyone was grieving and sobbing and chanting. A billionaire and his obscenely beautiful wife even promised to invest 100 million in its resurrection. Yet Maldon wondered if equally magnificent, munificent fiscal and emotional response could ever be given to drowned refugee children who washed from the dinghy at sea onto land. Children are historic too. Even cherubic and cathedral in their ecclesiastical influence. By lifting her chest and squeezing her eyes shut, she refused to cry over the 850-plus-years-old cement artifact constructed to celebrate pedophilia amongst the virgin priests. She had been there once. For her, it was like being inside a colossal kaleidoscope, rotating her in and out of flying buttresses, communal wafers, rose windows. She forced the backlog of tears from exiting her tear ducts.

She simply wouldn't allow the beloved church to behave like a sweat bee, feeding off the salinity of her sadness.

After a brief period of waiting in the hospital room, a team of surgeons and nurses and residents formed a half circle in front of her hospital chair. They all gawked at her like a Mona Lisa painting who was in a semi-desperate need of a heart operation. The doctor who spoke to her was an older, gray-haired man who spoke fluent Italian, English, and, as one of the nurses even emphasized, "Spanish." He may be a polyglot, but both the planet Neptune and Maldon thought he was an idiot who loved to hear the mellifluous tones of his own inexhaustible voice and existence.

DR. BANANA: You may take as long as you need to make a decision about an exceptional cardiologist. It's very wise and very important to have an excellent cardiologist. I highly recommend Dr. Orange. Dr. Grape wasn't a good fit for you because she spent too much time greasing her elbows. Dr. Kiwi has a pregnant wife who smokes fresh marijuana through a glass pipe. Do you like glass pipes? They are extraordinarily phallic. I think the company that built it didn't have men in mind. You see, we men like things less virtuous. I mean vitreous. It's less cold. We don't like to put things in our mouths that are cold. I am, by nature, not homophobic. I am an American doctor, you see. And I speak such good Italian.

	And my purses here—
MALDON:	Your what?
DR. BANANA:	My nurses.
MALDON:	You said purses.
DR. BANANA:	I did not. I can tell you that I like to put my cellphone in a fruit basket before I operate. My subgingival team here—
MALDON:	Your what?
DR. BANANA:	I mean, my surgical team here can confirm. We like to play this game called Whoever Touches It First—
MALDON:	I'm here to talk about the valve replacement surgery?
DR. BANANA:	Surgery is very safe in this modern era. If we don't operate on you today, you won't die, but tomorrow you might.
MALDON:	What time tomorrow?
DR. BANANA:	Excuse me?
MALDON:	You said tomorrow I might die. I just want to know what time I might die so I could sort of emotionally be prepared for it? It's like if I know what I'm having for breakfast, I might change my mind about what I might have for lunch. You understand?
DR. BANANA:	What I'm trying to say is that it's not very urgent yet, but it is extremely urgent.
MALDON:	What is urgent?
DR. BANANA:	Your heart surgery!
MALDON:	Ah, that. I thought we were talking about you getting dental floss.

DR. BANANA:	Why?
MALDON:	For you mentioned gum.
DR. BANANA:	I did not say any such thing.
MALDON:	Subgingival team.
DR. BANANA:	I meant surgical team, for Pete's sake.
MALDON:	Alright. Alright.
DR. BANANA:	Any other questions?
MALDON:	I think drinking blood thinner every day would diminish the quality of my life.
DR. BANANA:	It's just one fucking pill.
MALDON:	For the rest of my fucking life.

She didn't know what system to trust. Was the doctor making money off pharmaceutically enhanced surgery, i.e. surgical operations that would make patients dependent on pills? In a medicated system, Maldon thought, of course, one pill or thirty pills entering the bloodstream of the human body made no difference. It reminded her of an article she'd read in the newspaper a very long time ago. Maybe twenty years ago. The article was about a young drunk driver in his early twenties who killed a wealthy couple's sixteen-year-old daughter. The judge asked the couple how much money they wanted from the young man or how long should he be shackled. Or what was their ideal punishment for him? They told the judge that they did not want too much money. Just enough to live on. Every day for the rest of the young man's life, they asked that he must write a $1 check addressed to their daughter (her full name, for instance) and mail it postally every single day until he died. The young man complied. Drinking blood thinner daily made her medically incarcerated the same way, Maldon thought.

She was tired of different subliminal prison systems, especially since she hadn't killed anyone with a vehicle while drunk.

MALDON:	All we want are tests. May we have an echocardiogram, complete pulmonary function—
DR. BANANA:	No, no, no.
MALDON:	And a carotid duplex, angiogram, and an appointment with a cardiologist?
DR. BANANA:	Absolutely not.
MALDON:	Why not?
DR. BANANA:	It's absurd. You don't need any of those tests before an open-heart operation.

When they left Cloud City there was a hole the size of an expanding galaxy in Maldon's chest. It was a hole born out of familial isolation. Planet Neptune drove her to Cloud City and even drank good coffee with her, but the city itself made her feel damaged or even underappreciated somehow. She felt terribly undone, alone. There was a dark, abysmal hole in her ontological heart that could not be repaired or replaced with a valve-replacement operation. They passed miles of cornfields. Even from a distance, the headlights of a corn harvester or grain excavator plowing in the dark as it stripped miles of stalks seemed like a page out of a comic book. She felt very sad that she did not pass away on the East Coast. If she had died, she wouldn't have been confronted with this obliterating sense of sequestration and seclusion. However, optimistic Planet Neptune had a different idea about life post-surgery. A cheerful, buoyant one that was too inconsistent with Maldon's present state of mind or how she unraveled her existence.

NEPTUNE: The quality of your life will greatly improve after surgery.

MALDON: No, it won't.

NEPTUNE: Having a non-leaking heart will help your mental health as well. All of your existential problems are linked to this broken faucet that leaks
all of your vitality. Your buoyancy, your brio,
your verve, your vim, your vigor.

MALDON: Oh, fuck off.

NEPTUNE: Please.

MALDON: It won't change the way I feel about life.

NEPTUNE: You can't possibly know what you haven't experienced before.

MALDON: Clearly, you don't understand the circumference
of my imagination.

NEPTUNE: Surely, I don't have to. Just look at the inescapable biology of it. If you didn't have to get up every two seconds to mop up the leakage, it would
make it less laborious, and you would actually
enjoy living more. Don't argue with me. Agree
with me for once.

MALDON: And what if I do?

NEPTUNE: We would be on the same side.

MALDON: No.

NEPTUNE: Because I am Planet Neptune and I said so.
And, due to synchronous rotation, my fourteen
moons also agree with me. Especially Galatea,
Naiad, Despina and Thalassa.

MALDON: What about Proteus?

NEPTUNE: His polyhedronic mind is sometimes too dark,

and he may, occasionally and ellipsoidally, har-
monize with your way of thinking. Also, he is
protean.

MALDON: Doesn't mean he's unreliable.

NEPTUNE: I don't get it. Would you want someone to be on
your side?

MALDON: Not if they arrive from a specious place.

NEPTUNE: You don't want irrational fidelity?

MALDON: I want Larissa's alliance.

NEPTUNE: She is Poseidon's mistress.

MALDON: So?

Even though Planet Neptune had taken each chicken out for its
elimination ritual that morning, when they returned home that
evening from Cloud City, their football players had shat quite
a bit in their shadowboxes and nearly everywhere around the
house. Neptune chased them around the Airbnb with a bottle
of bleach, soap, and disinfectant. The odor was the most griev-
ous, involuntary thing. It nearly drove them insane.

NEPTUNE: Salt! Please cook something to get rid of this stench.

MALDON: Do you see how red their poop is? We should
stop feeding them Cheetos.

For three hours, Maldon slaved away in the kitchen. She butch-
ered one of the offensive linemen because linemen were more
dispensable and, because they moved less rigorously, they were
bound to object less than their counterparts (tight ends or running backs), their thighs were less muscular and, as a result,
more likely to be tender. Tender fowls were better than chewy
ones. At least from the human perspective. Before slaughtering

one for lunch, she turned to the eleven gallinaceous football players in their post-yoga stances and asked which one was willing to sacrifice itself for the team. The chickens somnambulated around each other like bowling balls with three holes at the center of their hearts. They rolled around each other hoping that an extra bounce or vibration would knock a random one out of alignment and that it would have no choice but to face its unfortunate fate. Take off your helmets, Maldon commanded. They shook their fat poultry asses. The intensity of their exertion elevated and hoisted their cushioned hats in the air. When they leaped and landed, it looked like the entire Airbnb was galvanized by a seizure of hollowed-out cannon balls. Maldon grabbed one by dipping her middle finger, index, and thumb into its thoracic holes. Sorry, Kwame Harris, but I've got to wring your neck, pluck your fancy feathers, and toss you in the boiler. You bounced out of alignment, and it simply means that you were ineffective. You don't have the discipline or fortitude to contain those savage, wild pass rushers. One down; ten to go, Maldon tallied in sotto voce.

In the midst of monitoring the baking conditions of her labor, the planet Mercury, who was deeply gay, who was gayer than Oscar Wilde but less gay than Hong Seok-Cheon, called Maldon and said that he was in the vicinity and wanted to come for a visit.

MALDON: Come, come. I am baking some chicken soaked in hoisin and fish sauce. And sautéing cabbage in salt and baked Yukon potatoes in fine butter. I even baked rice in mountain spring water.

MERCURY: At what temperature?

MALDON: Does it matter?

MERCURY: I don't have a cut-off point.

MALDON: What does that mean?

MERCURY: If it's over a certain degree I'll come. I'll come!

MALDON: Three-hundred-and-fifty-five degrees.

MERCURY: That's odd. Why not 360 degrees, like a protractor?

MALDON: I wanted 369, but it only moves in increments of five.

MERCURY: A travesty.

MALDON: (*To the potatoes*) I know Notre Dame just collapsed, but are you ready to come out of the oven?

MERCURY: I don't think they can respond.

MALDON: What if they want to stay longer and can't voice their desire?

MERCURY: What if they don't want to be browner or crispier?

MALDON: You see my point? (*To the potatoes*) Are you ready to come out?

MERCURY: Tell your potatoes this for me: I know you are gay, potatoes, but keep on going straight.

MALDON: These potatoes are not going anywhere, and they are not gay.

MERCURY: They belong in the nightshade family. Of course, they're queer.

MALDON: I think the parsnips would be deeply offended.

In Maldon's *somnia a Deo missa* (dreams sent by God), there was nudity and the sea and the mirror that reflected the nudity of the sea. Then there was Maldon and another inventor. She was hyperintelligent. A vigilant soul who could cut through glass with one thought. She could see her intelligence reflected in the rim of her glass. When they were standing in sand, they could see that the sea and the waves were huge, combating gravity. The waves were outcompeted by gravity, which explained the unexpected height of the sea. There were many boats placed intermittently on the tops of the waves as if they were Cheerios floating on a cereal bowl made of blue milk. The inventor sprayed perfume into her mouth so that her breath would smell dizzyingly good. When Maldon woke up she learned that she was a quarter of a century younger than Rae Armantrout.

The first thunderstorm arrived in Cloud, carrying on its back an electric current of desire. Rain compromised itself by being fluent in falling apart as soon as it reached the surface of cement, grass, and whatnot. In the midst of falling, one string of rain held the hand of another raindrop. They were tied pluvially to the hip before their splattered release. Before they were forced to grow apart. Sitting at the dining table with Planet Neptune, Maldon watched this leakage from the foggy window of her late afternoon existence.

NEPTUNE: The fist of rain.
MALDON: Liquid pugilist.
NEPTUNE: On my planet, we call it Poseidon's tears.
MALDON: Apt.
NEPTUNE: Does it feel as if our days lately are like a vacation from life?
MALDON: This interlude before my surgery.
NEPTUNE: Yes.

MALDON: If only eighty-six percent of our lives were like
           this.
NEPTUNE: It would be ideal, wouldn't it?
MALDON: Yes, it would.

Near Neptune's plate of cabbage and marinated lineman, basically Kwame Harris on a plate, Maldon noticed a business
card with a green strip running like a stripper or a ticker at its
bottom. She picked it up and studied it.

NEPTUNE: Your surgeon has an MD and a PhD. The next
           time you see him you should ask him what his
           PhD. was in.
MALDON: That's a good idea.
NEPTUNE: My mother's thesis was on ectopic pregnancy.
           That's when the fetus attaches itself outside of
           the mother's uterus. For instance, the stomach.
MALDON: What about the kidney?
NEPTUNE: I'm not a doctor, but sure. It's hard to create in-
           telligent, exoplanetary life outside of the moth-
           er's uterine solar system.
MALDON: It is. She wrote it when you were with her in
           Ireland?
NEPTUNE: Yes. Impressively, she won a huge prize for it.
           But imagine how fucked up you must have to be.
MALDON: To be geographically deficient enough that you
           missed your mother's tubby spacecraft?
NEPTUNE: That's just a bad start to life, don't you think?
MALDON: For that fertilized egg?
NEPTUNE: My gynecologist mother has brought some of
           these babies into the world from time to time.

MALDON: I try to imagine the embryo clinging to the side
            of the roof with its embryonic fingers as a torna-
            do blows through.
NEPTUNE: Instead of being inside its mother's basement?
            Sealed away from glass windows?
MALDON: Yeah. Something like that.

As she was decapitating the second gallinaceous football cock
with a serrated knife, Maldon thought: yes, it's true. The universe was giving her what she wanted: to die. The surgeon was
going to stop her heart, and for three hours or so, she would
be a carcass with a soul that would be circumvented and cir-
culated out of her, like a library book on an interlibrary loan.
The heart-lung machine was like a river waiting for her. As the
machine breathed for her, her blood would be Japanese tennis
player Naomi Osaka traveling up the length and width of the
tennis court with those muscular thighs of hers, bouncing the
tennis ball of her life, keeping it in court as long as possible. As
soon as it exited the court, she would permanently be dead.
She held the headless cock over the sink, its floriated blood
spilling all over as she studied the cock's lifeless form. Its head
was in a strainer. Although she would never equate beheading
a chicken with rearranging a bouquet of flowers in a vase, it felt
like it. Trimming the veiny stems, seeing all the verdant leaves
falling into the sink, and adding water to its soon-to-be deceased floral body in a glass vase. It was both messy and clean.
Taking life out of a life for biological or aesthetical consumption. It all felt violent to Maldon. Every aspect of life felt that
way to her, including the art of dying. She dipped the headless
body of the cock in boiling water to make the plucking more

efficient. She loved how methodically efficient it was, the violence of its calmness. Plucking the wet and post-steamed feathers from the flaccid skin effortlessly, with the efficiency of her fingers and thumb as they worked in unity to move from one armpit section of the cock to the next, Maldon felt as if her hand were designed to kiss the air with each plucking breath. Later she rubbed Maldon salt onto their armpits and inner and outer thighs and inside their guts and organs and rib cages. Salting made the chicken less odorous. Would they reciprocate her fatal affection? She turned her head over to where the shadowboxes were. Two were vacant, the void from the decapitation and ingestion. Slowly, Planet Neptune and Maldon were making their way through by emptying the shadowboxes of their shadows and replacing indifference with Darwinism. She imagined God carving the insides of each planet with a spoon and swallowing the contents of each domesticated celestial body as if he were a child enjoying each scoop of his half-gaseous, half-rocky ice cream. What she was doing with the chickens was quite similar, Maldon thought.

NEPTUNE: Do you think the meat was a bit tough?
MALDON: It was a little chewy, I think.

When the afternoon had fallen asleep, Maldon found herself reading a book by a Swiss psychoanalyst on the functions of the unconsciousness. In the midst of it all, an email from Southwest arrived in her inbox to inform her that her mother's twenty-four months were nearly over. If she didn't use her Southwest points in two months, she would lose them. She tried to sign into her mother's account to buy two tickets on some random days in September, but the system kept kicking her out. Enervated and frustrated, she called her mother for assistance.

MALDON: Could you call the airline and ask them to buy these tickets on your behalf for me so we can save these points?

MOTHER: Sure.

MALDON: Request the month of September. From Su 890 to Denver. It's the only month when you can maximize the points you can save.

MOTHER: Anything else?

MALDON: Don't buy it for the months of June and July.

MOTHER: Why?

MALDON: It's when you travel to Tokyo, Mother.

MOTHER: Right. Right.

MALDON: The others cancelled their flights.

MOTHER: Your siblings never booked their flights in the first place.

MALDON: That's a shame. You'll be going to Tokyo alone.

MOTHER: I won't be sad.

MALDON: Why did they cancel their plans?

MOTHER: They didn't really say.

MALDON: What do you think?

MOTHER: Your brother lost twenty pounds, Butterfly lost ten, but Ngọc struggled with the diet and couldn't. Because she didn't lose enough weight in time, they all doomed themselves out of a vacation.

MALDON: I see.

MOTHER: Your brother is jobless so he can afford to eat nearly nothing. Butterfly has a treadmill she can hop onto when her kids take naps. But Ngọc's job is sedentary, and with so much work stress, she wants to resort to food for comfort. And it's really hard to lose weight on demand. Her bedroom is closer to the kitchen, and when temptation is a thin wall away, it's easy to snack on carbs and salt, which retain the water and make her look more inflated than she actually is. You can lose ten pounds from water weight, which is an optical illusion for all dieters. It's hard to not eat for eighteen hours. To skip breakfast and lunch. Even for me, I can skip breakfast, but lunch? Lunch is my biggest meal. It's hard to renovate the bedroom so it won't be closer to the kitchen. She would need to break down her huge house—

MALDON: It's not the house, Mother.

MOTHER: What is it then?

MALDON: She really loves food.

MOTHER: So?

MALDON: Why would she alter her lifestyle in a way that removes and confiscates the one thing she loves most about life? No wonder her diet can't and shouldn't work.

MOTHER: She loves food that much?

MALDON: Yeah.

MOTHER: I love food too.

MALDON: Not like Ngọc. And if you resist food as efficiently as you do, then you don't love food that much. You can only have power over something that you don't love. Love makes one submissive.

MOTHER: Am I submissive?

MALDON: Mother, you are an elevator that won't allow anyone to push their desired floor button.

MOTHER: What does that mean?

MALDON: It means taking the stairs a cunt.

MOTHER: What is a cunt? Can you spell it out for me?

MALDON: *K* as in kicking.

MOTHER: *K* as in what?

MALDON: *K* as in KICKING. *A* as in amnesia, *N* as in Nutella, and *T* as in toothpaste. *K-A-N-T.*

MOTHER: I'm not the head judge for The Scripps National Spelling Bee, you know, daughter.

MALDON: Well, you asked me to. You said, "spell it out for me."

MOTHER: I meant gently.

MALDON: I am gentle. How gentle do you want me to be? Kant.

MOTHER: There. There. That wasn't so hard.

MALDON: Kant. Kant was a German philosopher who argued that an elevator has time, space, and causation, but it's so emotionally defective that we can't ever know if an elevator has any enigma left for us to explore or if it has so much ontological enigma that, when it moves up and down, we think it might be capable of moving sideways too, emotionally, of course. Just to be clear, it's not impossible physically. That's what a bullet train or subway is for. Kant also believed that we should never be skeptical when we step into an elevator. He blamed Hume for feeding

humans the seeds of distrust. Basically, he was a
religiously reduced Christian who wanted Christ
to take the elevator up to his crucifix.

MOTHER: Why didn't he take the elevator like Kant wanted to? If someone wants you to do something,
you should submit to their desire.

MALDON: Because Jesus was a carpenter.

MOTHER: So?

MALDON: He loved wood.

MOTHER: Like the way Ngọc loves her tiramisu.

MALDON: Exactly. That's what the crucifix is for.

MOTHER: To get his timber fix.

MALDON: I bet when they nailed him to—

MOTHER: What kind of wood was it?

MALDON: The crucifix?

MOTHER: Cypress? Cedar?

MALDON: Birch because it rhymes with church. I bet when
they nailed him to birch, I bet he got a little bit
of pleasure out of it.

MOTHER: When you are being tortured, pain is pain,
daughter.

Before climbing into bed Maldon turned to the remaining nine
football players. They all gathered around her like the Milky
Way. She turned to them and asked, "Who wants to be next?"
Like a quiet choir of birds, they made no response. Maldon
grabbed the first one she saw. She didn't care if it was a quarterback or the receiver; she needed one quickly because she
had gotten so sleepy all of a sudden that she just simply wanted
to crawl into bed. By removing all of her belongings from her

navy blue Tommy Hilfiger backpack, she could tackle the next task: she cut a hole the size of a woman's nipple out of the bottom, inserted the hen into the backpack, and zipped her up with the zipper grip on both sides so that her head and gullet were exposed and visible to the world. Then she hung the hen up on the coat hook near the main the door. The poor hen's extensively bulging eyeballs and protuberant nose faced the desolate, lawn-chair-less backyard behind her. Maldon took one last looked at her and gently patted the backpack's protruding stomach. The apprehensive hen rolled her eyes back and forth like marbles on a glass plate, as if begging forgiveness for a crime she didn't commit. In the early morning, when the chickens had returned to their prison rooms, their shadowboxes, Maldon got up to relieve herself. Even in her deep soporific state, when she turned toward the coat hook to observe, briefly, the current state of her affixed hen and noticed a small pile of yellow shit like a splatter of paint on the wood floor like a temporary art piece, she understood the hen's un-ornamental, primal fear. The hen knew its life was coming to a cul-de-sac. Shitting, like giving birth, was the hen's way of being God, activating her prehistoric, divine proclivity to act out her pent-up longing for expulsion. Shit was her Adam and Eve. The first man and first woman were bespattered on the Airbnb's wood floor. She nodded her head and climbed back into bed.

Hours later, Maldon was cooking in the kitchen. Boiling water was doing the Macarena, a kind of callisthenic leap, in the big aluminum pot.

MALDON: Look on the bright side. At least I didn't soak you in bleach. Now that white isn't a spiritually nor emotionally nor ontologically nor verbally nor substantially nor politically popular color anymore, you can be as yellow as you want. Doesn't it feel nicer and tastier without that extra sodium hypochlorite in you? The Black Lives Matter movement is basically saying, No more sodium hydroxide. No more calcium hypochlorite. No more. No more. There will be a time in the near future when I can't wring your neck anymore. That time hasn't come yet for you. So you are, basically, doomed.

NEPTUNE: (*Emerging from the bathroom*) Who are you talking to?

MALDON: The halfback.

NEPTUNE: Huh?

MALDON: Doak Walker.

NEPTUNE: I thought he was dead.

MALDON: *(Pointing to the boiled hen)* He is.

NEPTUNE: That's a hen. A she.

MALDON: Doak Walker was a she! And we are having her for dinner.

NEPTUNE: I thought Doak won the Heisman Trophy in 1948 for playing for SMU.

MALDON: You are not wrong. She was a golden egg. As golden as any golden egg can be.

NEPTUNE: But Doak wasn't an egg. Nor a hen. He was a very talented American football player.

MALDON: We are having Doak for lunch. That's that.

NEPTUNE: Alright alright. I just spoke to Bell Pepper.

MALDON: Who is that?

NEPTUNE: The nurse at Alpha UMi Aa Hospital.

MALDON: Yes, yes, her. What did she say?

NEPTUNE: She didn't say anything. I just scheduled an angiogram for you.

MALDON: Thank you. That's unforgivable.

NEPTUNE: What?

MALDON: What kind of mother names her child "Bell
Pepper"?

It took them a week to finish the first season of *Killing Eve*. Maldon had intense hedonistic tendencies and preferred to binge
everything, including watching the first season (and subsequent
seasons) of each television show within a twenty-four-hour window. She could simply flash them all in her head as if they were
distant galaxies: the supernatural, memory-wiping-gas-per-
suaded, or drowning-induced Brit Marling in the sci-fi/ para-
normal *The OA*, while traveling unconsciously and consciously
through parallel dimensions, flashing through the grandeur of
Russia like childhood amnesia and trauma as she gets semi-
fucked, as in tortured and semi-assassinated, as in half-deathed
by a computer-operated, voice-ish, telepathic-ish, oversized,
highly sexualized sea creature thing called an octopus; the clever,
un-casually Islamophobic British series *Bodyguard* with When-
God-Was-a-Woman Keeley Hawes commanding her martinet
MP position and her unexpected, but expected, weakness for
her opposing erogenous force of postpartum depression, co-
star Richard Madden in his masterful, protective display as
postwar police sergeant, gigolo-like bodyguard-y type, sexual
seclusion, or perversion (he did strangle the MP, post-coital-
ly and unintentionally, but still) and reverse power-dominance

provocation to reduce all of Britain's intelligent (but not MI5 or MI6) and not-so-intelligent women (everyone else) into drooling speechlessness and submission; Canadian sci-fi time-traveling *Travelers* and its post-apocalyptic, protocol-driven itinerants from the future taking morally unjustified (who needs consent in the future or past?) and justified (can be bypassed if it saves the world in the future), consent-less residency in the defective bodies of their twenty-first-century hosts, hosts with cerebral disabilities, heroin addiction, one the victim of domestic abuse married to a police officer, to name a few, as they attempt to prevent an atomic-like explosion that could wipe out half of the world's population by altering the DNA of history without history or other time-reprehensible travelers knowing that their DNA has been reformed or has been mismanaged; the "professorial," un-sangria-led, highly sophisticated eight-person team (hacker, forger, torturer, miners, etc.) of Álvaro Morte or "professorial" trained bank robbers who shouldn't humanly, emotionally, or corporeally fuck each other but do in Spanish roller-coaster drama *Money Heist* (previously named *La Casa de Papel*) to undermine, to idiotize, and to sexually, psychologically, and scientifically deride a female-spearheaded (Itziar Ituño), government-backed elite team of police officers by printing about two billion euros at Madrid's Royal Mint of Spain while quietly, deceptively, politically, ineloquently, dumbfoundedly, and semi-un-violently (at first) managing sixty-seven hostages; penetratingly-acted Sherlock by handsome Benedict Cumberbatch in *Sherlock*; in Canadian sci-fi crime drama *Continuum*, law enforcement officer or "protector" Kiera Cameron, in the highest state-of-the-art, bulletproofed, electromagnetic, polymeric, nano-synthesized, self-reparative, futuristic bodysuit, time-travels un-portently in Vancouver to chase after fugitive terrorists who are inmates from 2077 on death row who anachronistically escaped to 2012, in hopes of bringing them back to dystopic, corporatocratic 2077 to face their sentences; bored, non-gym-member, therapist-going Lucifer Morningstar (Tom Ellis), also known as the Devil, relinquishes his fancy throne as Emperor-of-Purgatory in order to live compassionately and co-run an exclusive, elite bar in LA with a (South African) demon (Lesley-Ann Brandt) while trying to help a detective (Lauren German), his Achilles' heel being to fall in love with her while they solve ineloquent murders in the American (tragic) comedy series with an unpredictable name, *Lucifer;* subtexted, unsubtexted, hyperintelligent, mischievously vindictive hacker Root (Amy Acker), seduces Dr. Shaw (Sarah Shahi) at the beginning of their Sapphic (but not yet revealed) courtship by wanting to torture her (soon-to-be) lover with a searingly hot iron before she is cerebrally and psychologically tortured in the most viciously artificial-intelligence style via drug-induced, quasi-infinite, hyper-real, theoretically-possibility-based simulation in the very un-narrowly designed subplot (this so-isolated plot) and in the most affluent state-of-the-art, computer-programed, supercomputed, Robinhood-esque, cyber-grounded crime drama (main plot) of *Person of Interest*; in *Blue Bloods*, morally uncorrupted police commissioner Frank Reagan (played by Tom Selleck) vanguards his equally morally uncorrupted, heroic, civic-happy, multigenerational family-run business into a Catholic entrail of lawyers, prayers, police officers, and detectives in a collective, remorselessly and fastidiously attended, once a week, exclusive family dinner that does not involve their un-lightly mourned, assassinated brother (son) and deceased

mother (wife); in a highly sensitized, Syrian-refugee-based political ethos, suave, exceptionally quick-witted, quick-minded,
pregnant London Detective Inspector (Carey Mulligan), in the
quadranted, feminist thriller *Collateral*, explores lucidly, deftly,
and diplomatically the underbelly of London's reprehensible,
politically sullied underworld where witness and assassin bring
more surprises than a burger stuffed in the back pocket of a
pizza deliveryman by playing her cards just right; lizardly in its
Edenic depth, *Death in Paradise* brings sand and homesickness to
the fictionaly landmass of Saint Marie in the Caribbean where
the killer(s) and suspects are invited by the detective in the last
five minutes or so of each episode for a casual group meeting
at which he fully narrates and explains before the suspects and
murderer(s), of course, how the killer committed his crime;
pimped by youthful, naive love, beguiled by expensive cellphones and shopping lifestyles, affluent underaged girls from
an aristocratic private high school are sought out and recruited
for prostitution by lewd businessmen in the highly controversial
six-part Italian teen drama *Baby*; *The Vietnam War* documenta-
ry; Ayelet Zurer plays the brilliant surgeon Dr. Yael Danon in
Israeli crime drama series *Hostages*, where she is coerced, not
quite, by men in masks into assassinating the prime minister in
exchange for the safety of her family—mainly her extremely
fallible, irresponsible, lame-duck husband and semi-egomani-
ac children—but the doctor fights back in a masterful, surgi-
cal-ninja style of skillful intelligence, procedural exploration,
sleight-of-hand maneuvering, and magnificently dexterous research; in a generous act of synchronicity and the most innoc-
uous display of soul transference—

ADMINISTRATOR:	Son of Israeli leader—
MALDON:	Who?
ADMINISTRATOR:	Samson.
MALDON:	Did he cut off his long, beautiful Afro hair again?
ADMINISTRATOR:	No. At any rate, his son, Dehi, your student.
MALDON:	My former student—
ADMINISTRATOR:	Yes, Dehi emailed me that the class has bought a gift for you and would like to mail it to you.
MALDON:	Oh, dear. Is it an ephemeral gift? If it is . . . I won't have an address to offer him.
ADMINISTRATOR:	I'll ask.

By calling her, the administrator at Westerlund (not one of the brightest stars or universities in the universe; it felt like 16,000 light-years from her lover, Earth) interrupted and snapped Maldon out of her fugue, her trancelike computation of her intimate membership with arithmetical reality in the last month or so as a million images and summarizations exponentially grew and reorbited the primary theater of her existence, which was her memory. Of reality. The kind of digital, enhanced reality that did not expose her to her own reality, which was her life outside of the not-so-live streaming mediums of Netflix, Amazon Prime, Hulu, HBO, and Kanopy. Yet, it wasn't hard for her to pick up where she had left off and return to the revenue of tallying the contents of her digital addiction:

—or heart-based consciousness substitution, an explicitly cold-hearted, workalcoholic business magnate (Jung Kyung-ho) becomes hypersensitive and romantically loving after a heart transplant in which he receives the heart of a kind police officer, which surprisingly allows him and his new heart to court the woman (Kim So-yeon) of his dreams in that most romantic South Korean comedy drama *Falling For Innocence*, etc. Etc. Etc. Etc. Despite his extremely gelidlike, Nepturian, interchangeable gender condition, Planet Neptune's visual consumption was balanced and mild in comparison to her contemporaries such as Maldon. When asked which of these wild and extraordinarily compelling shows Maldon loved the most, she wouldn't be able to tell herself or anyone. And, yet or not yet, she did wonder what her life would be like if it were a reality TV show for God or some extraterrestrial being. Would it be like those highly imaginative TV series she could alpha or not alphanumerically rattle off, or was her life a series of boring, random snippets of interrupted scenes and ambient hours and static cut from an abandoned 16 mm vintage film reel and reassembled to look somewhat like her shoddy life? More directly, was her life a poorly made film? Was this the reason why she had had a bad heart since childhood? Most specifically, was she a poorly made, poorly budgeted film? Like *Evan Almighty* or *Transformers: Age of Extinction* (as if the movie, portentous by the suggestion of its title, wished for its own extinction). And did God help her co-write her life at all? Or was she the primary culprit of her design? Maldon did want to cut her life out of her life or her life out of God's (seemingly) infinite film reel. She did like the language of 16 mm. She did like the cinematography of chance. She did like God at some point when he was a filmmaker of other people's lives instead of hers. When she was teaching at Westerlund at the time when her heart was breaking down and she told God "CUT NOW" and "Close Production of Maldon Interstellar NOW" and God said an emphatic "NO!", God, the producer of everything, had intervened. It felt more and more now that God had taken over the messy project of life. He was the designer, the producer, the editor (the primary editor), screenwriter, art director, cinematographer, production designer; apart from being the music supervisor of her consciousness, God had taken over everything.

Her last name was Interstellar, which meant "placed in between stars." With his warm, non-biotechnological words, he was placing her somewhere in between his own stars. How could she not want to be loved in some significant way? From an empirical standpoint alone, Maldon knew the strongest muscle in her body was breaking down at an exponential rate. When she took Doak Walker and not Luke Skywalker out of the refrigerator, she knew she had weakened massively. Doak only weighted 3.6 pounds, and the rectangular glass baking dish could be placed generously at 3.1 pounds. Since Neptune and Maldon had eaten through almost half of baked Doak, the whole container came to less than five pounds, but gripping it at an awkward 67 degrees while she transferred it into a Tupperware container for less than a minute wore her heart out. Exhausted her. She walked to the sofa to take a breather. Every aspect of life enervated her. Taking a laundry basket half full with freshly washed hand and bath towels upstairs to the bathroom, holding up her cellphone while she texted in bed, frying rice in a frying pan with a plastic spatula, shampooing her hair and lifting her hands up to scrub, lifting the pint of water into the brewing machine to make coffee for Planet Neptune, taking a plate out of the dishwasher, and other minor tasks, such as walking to and fro, all enervated her, drained her of piss and vinegar. Almost every single task that the human body performed required the heart muscle. She heard the buzzer in the basement. She pulled herself off the sofa and descended the stairs and carried a load of laundry up. When the surgeon told her that she could not cook nor do laundry, Maldon almost cried. Of the few ontological tasks she loved about her life, the greatest would be the joy of cooking and folding clothes into origami shapes. She starched and folded Neptune's articles of clothing according to one of Professor Jun Mitani's 3D algorithmic origamic techniques: his nightgowns into origami spheres, her shirts into triangles of whipped cream, his pants into Christmas ornaments, her handkerchiefs into an ellipse with ten flaps, her bath towel into a curved plate, his socks into pears, her ties into apples, his bras into a column embossed with circles, and her undergarments into six windmills. She loved the shapes of fabric life. In here, there was no future. No past tense. No ontological denial. Finished with folding, she carried the laundry basket filled with geometrical materials to Neptune's room. She knocked on his door. When she heard a soft groan, she pushed herself inside. The planet was sleeping on his side, a Le Verrier length of hydrocarbonic blankets toppling all over her. Maldon was unable to even make out a single helium-sized whisp of his existence. She came closer and lifted the blankets.

MALDON: Nep?

NEPTUNE: Ugggh . . .

MALDON: What's wrong.

NEPTUNE: My period came.

MALDON: Oh, what a bummer.

NEPTUNE: I ran out of pads, and my cramps are terrible.

MALDON: Oh no.

NEPTUNE: I can contain the hydrogen and ammonia leakage. . . .

MALDON: With what?

NEPTUNE: This Airbnb pillow.

MALDON: I see.

NEPTUNE: Walk to the pharmacy with me?

MALDON: I'm too tired.

And just like that Neptune was on her toes and out of the door
in search of more maxi pads. Maldon watched him step onto
the sidewalk and silently make her un-telescopic way into the
remotest region of the galaxy. His faint ring system not guiding
the way, the music of her orbital resonances moving like an
iPod through his body. She was a planet on the verge of his
retrograde cycle. Despite being so astronomically cold all the
time, this sea king star wasn't at all impervious to the biblical
sea monster of menstruation. It happened to everyone, including straight white men, even non-cis planets, even to a gen-
der-fluctuating sphere still in an ambiguous, hermaphroditic
sexual transit, even if everything stopped becoming methane
gas. She imagined her walking down the boulevard, leaking his
unscented combustible gas, walking alone, not unlike a vam-
pire on a skateboard. Her blue hair casting nebulous streaks
of shadows onto the cement ground, onto the spines of some

of the magnificent trees in the universe, trees such as quaking aspen, bristlecone pine, and, she imagined, even for him, the air heavy like Prometheus. Maldon understood, even if she did have a Methuselah tree inside her, buried 11,000 feet above the sea level of her desire, that she wouldn't know what it would be like for Planet Neptune to be on her period. She tried to sympathize. Maldon prepared a liquid hydrogen flask infused with scent of evergreen and tetrahedral ginger to help stabilize Neptune's mega-scale, extreme internal and external climate changes. When he returned from the pharmacy, she reclined in bed with him, placed and pressed the medicinal flask against her stomach without bending his five dusty optical rings and ring arcs.

MALDON: Try to keep the flask straight up. I tried to plug the sprout with some foam, but just in case it leaks. This will help control the oceans of temperament and semitones combating your internal planetary system.

NEPTUNE: I'll keep that in mind.

MALDON: When you are not in pain anymore, we should book our next Airbnb place. Our time here is coming to an end in three days.

NEPTUNE: Done.

While Neptune fell asleep, Maldon studied the light floating through the French window, bouncing its shadow against the wall painted gray across from the bed. Light always had the ability to fashion portals out of flat, inanimate surfaces, but these windows were an optical illusion providing no exit or entrance to another world or an alternate universe. Aggravated by this incapacitated foresight, Maldon closed her eyes and fell asleep.

On an occasion that was obscenely too beautiful, Planet Neptune and Maldon Uubered to Best Buy to purchase a personal teleporter device. His current one hadn't malfunctioned yet but was on its way, and Maldon insisted that it was better to have a backup than to be yanked out of commission. Teleporter devices remained popular still because they allowed researchers to hook their subconsciousness to The Ru Oracle, which allowed optical, noetic nerves to collect scientific thoughts as they travelled across collective time. Even a prophetess could be born from data. Even data could be an alphanumeric entity, a collective analytic clairvoyant. Even data could be a student of time and a mistress to a billion combinations and recombinations, a Whore Einstein within an Einstein. The question had always been, for all human linkers and thinkers: Why become a sex worker when a machine could explore infinite sexual inquiries in its sleep, probing and scrutinizing fieldwork with all of its priapic eyes closed? Obviously, an Orphic machine can outperform the human on a non-waterbed, but a personalized teleporter forced the machine to be a scientist, scholar, and sex worker of itself and possibly of dinosaurs without legs from the Mesozoic Era. Through the help of a teleporter, the human consciousness had the capacity to access the back door of time at a very precise point in time, allowing humans to leap from machine to machine, from one sexual reproductive organ to the next, without AI knowing and adapting its exoatmospheric structure and apparatus to the freeway or sperm bank of reality. A scholar without a big brother was like a sister with an apple strudel. A strudel was a pastry born in 1696 and invented for the Habsburg Empire. It was designed to symbolize a whirlpool of endless possibilities.

Perhaps this was Neptune's scholarly dream, but regardless, they had Uubered to Best Buy, and Neptune was very much in need of a new laptop to work on her research paper. Maldon had no choice but to oblige. They wandered about before nailing the laptop department with their eager, studious eyes. A Best Buy associate with cheekbone-length hair the color of peach strudel approached her asking if she needed any assistance. Maldon mumbled something incoherent, and the associate excused herself from her presence. Meanwhile, from her peripheral eye, Planet Neptune was eyeing a Chromebook, and Maldon came closer to her.

MALDON: You noticed that associate over there?

NEPTUNE: Yeah?

MALDON: Will you ask her if she likes collard greens?

NEPTUNE: She looks quite womanly and femininely.

MALDON: What if she doesn't like brussels sprouts?

NEPTUNE: My brother is very good at detecting such.

MALDON: Will you furtively take a picture of her, text it to your brother, and ask him if she previously loved collard greens?

NEPTUNE: That's so verdant of you.

MALDON: If I take a picture of her and—

NEPTUNE: Still so verdant.

MALDON: I wish I were a type of vegetable so I could ask her out.

NEPTUNE: I wish we both had loved brussels sprouts and collard greens and penises.

MALDON: One in front and one in the back?

NEPTUNE: Collapsible.

MALDON: Like wheels on an airplane?

NEPTUNE: You mean wings?

MALDON: Wheels like nipples, tucked in after liftoff. And automatically untucked upon landing.

NEPTUNE: Is it calcium or vitamin D? Have you forgotten the artifacts of my nightshade family? The textural quality of my verdanthood?

The associate was at least a quarter of a football field away from both of them while Maldon stole shy, stealthy glances of her from a healthy distance. What was it about her that was so appealing to Maldon?

MALDON: I'm interested in her, but she might not be so brussels-sprout friendly.

NEPTUNE: You usually go for collard green-type women.

MALDON: Rarely sexually osteoporotic beings.

NEPTUNE: Exactly. So what is the difference here?

MALDON: I love how wide her shoulders are. Most collard green women's shoulders are rarely that broad. They remind me of my mother's wood hangers for very light autumn silk dresses that could float in and out of the sea. And her broad wrists, masculine in the most elegant way, like they are thick and sultry, like they haven't experienced starvation, malnutrition, famine, or food shortage ever in their youthful, short life.

NEPTUNE: You a-r-e fucked. If you ask if she had ever been a lettuce, she would be offended.

MALDON: And if she had been, she would be even more affronted because—

NEPTUNE: You would have insulted her deft camouflage.

MALDON: I am fucked either way.

NEPTUNE: Just ask her out.

MALDON: No.

NEPTUNE: No?

MALDON: She might be too young for me.

NEPTUNE: She might be older than she looks. I noticed she did have on a thick coat of chlorophyll.

MALDON: Perhaps to hide her calcium deficiency.

NEPTUNE: Would you be deeply disappointed if she does have some cyanobacteria essence in her?

MALDON: Perhaps not.

NEPTUNE: Regardless, besides the hanger motif, why are you drawn to her wide shoulders?

MALDON: In *Little Red Riding Hood,* Little Red asks her wolfly grandmother why her premolars are so mammoth. 'The better to eat you,' was her reply. Do you recall? Well, a woman with broad shoulders, to answer you: the better to hold me.

NEPTUNE: This doesn't explain your fixation on her broad wrists.

MALDON: Do you think she can hear us?

NEPTUNE: This conversation?

MALDON: Yeah?

NEPTUNE: With the way you're behaving, anyone can hear us.

MALDON: Well, you kept accusing me of being transverdant—

NEPTUNE: Well, you are.

MALDON: Well, in that case, I want to convert my transver-
          dancy into a date.

NEPTUNE: Just fucking ask her. If she has many single stems,
          then ask her if—

MALDON: She would tuck it in or you could tuck it in for
          her like—

NEPTUNE: Like tucking your hair behind your ears.

MALDON: I love long hair, you know.

NEPTUNE: And I love ears because I don't have any.

Every day since being here, Planet Neptune had asked her
to wake him up early so that she could get more work and
research done, but each day the planet had a hard time
cracking open his blue, methane eyes. The average number
of hours it took for the planet to be up and about, drinking
coffee and diving into some baked strudel Maldon had made
for her, was about six hours, one-fourth of Earth's day. She
was aware that it took approximately 164.79 years for the
planet to orbit around the Sun and had expected him to be
slow in starting her day, but six hours was clearly abominable.
It blew through most of anyone's day and made it impossible
for Maldon to do anything mildly productive with him. She
started by shaking her twice, yanking off his protective atmospheric blanket, and then rang the violent manual clock that
shook and shrieked like a *Vulpes vulpes,* or red fox. When that
didn't work, she tapped on her door with a binaural knuck-
le blaze that could raise the temperature of any planet by
two-hundred degrees Celsius, yet the planet refused to stir.
Maldon realized that if he wanted to wake up, he would find

a way to do so, and she forsook the Neptune-hired matutinal vocation entirely.

After they exited Best Buy with an HP laptop, Maldon discovered that her lover from afar had fallen ill. All of Westerlund had fallen under a massive viral spell. Everyone and everything was falling from the freeway of vigor at a decimal rate. Planet Saturn's throat was bruised with inflammation, and she could hardly utter a single word. On the Uuber ride back home, the conservative, scandalized eyes of the Uuber driver were bulging in disbelief. Maldon decided to tell Saturn a story to keep her atmospheric sanity alive.

MALDON: At the beginning of the universe, God and Satan were two homosexual arsonists and lovers who were happy and overjoyed to keep their homosexual hysterics and tendencies to a minimum by playing with incendiaries. One of their favorite things to do in a spaceless medium and in a timeless space was to make fireworks by blowing up stars, just for kicks. It was their private Chinese New Year. But Satan got bored with God and with himself, and he grew tired of fucking just God, so he decided to go off on his own. He was interested in a barbecued rib marinated in thyme and rosemary that God pulled out of a man's thoracic cavity. The rib had a name: Adam. God, being God, was deeply offended by his lover's new video console, and when Satan abandoned him, God whispered to a few misguided Christians that sodomy was a form of biblical terrorism in order to make sure that the act got banned in a fancy book bigotorially. And so it was—

NEPTUNE: I think we are here.

The driver pulled his van up to their Airbnb, and as they stepped off, like Grant Wood's 1930 *American Gothic*, both Neptune and Maldon waved goodbye. Inside, she left the planet to explore his new laptop and conclude her conversation with her invalid lover from afar. She promised she would continue the narration of the origin of the universe as soon as she lobotomized one football player in a glass baking dish filled with fish sauce, ginger, hoisin sauce, pepper, and soy sauce. They had finished consuming Doak or whatever was left of his thigh, and they were ready for the next oblation. Most of the team's players were taking an afternoon nap inside of their shadowboxes, and Maldon almost did not have the heart to pull one out of its tranquil amnesia for the guillotine, but Neptune was on her period, and he needed the iron. Even iron pills could not compensate for Neptune's rapid leakage. Naturally, she yanked the center, Maurkice Pouncey, from his warm nest and placed him in her arms. In one swift move, the way elegant, psychopathic Villanelle cradled that orphaned, pizza-faced boy in her arms at the hospital before snapping his head to mercy kill him, Maldon applied the same technique to this Maurkice. She laid him in the sink while she peeled ginger. Grating the ginger with a cheese grater, she grew unpredictably fatigued, and in seconds there were massive bags under her eyes. Have I always been this tired, but it's just now that it's became unbearable? Maldon asked herself. She quickly abandoned the task, left lifeless Maurkice in the sink, and washed her hands. She walked to the living room and sat down on the sofa to rest. She could see parts of Cloud from this angle. She noticed from the window a small blue flag impaled in the throat in a patch of grass blowing quietly in the wind, trembling unspeakably. This scene, due to its parallel vulnerability, reminded her of a moment in her past. It was her time at Westerlund. If she were honest with herself, there was one student at Westerlund who wanted to be closer to her, who valued her awkward, intense teaching methodology, who tried to become closer by asking her one day while her shoulders were stiff, her heart was bolted shut with diamonds and titanium, about her intergalactic travel to Betelgeuse. She had kept herself cold from him because she didn't want him to love her and to see the virtue in her existence since if one person cared enough about if she lived or died, she might lose the will to exercise the power of suicide. The power of anti-discontinuance. She thought of Claudia Rankine. She read somewhere on the internet that her favorite word is "Here"; it made her wonder what her own favorite word was. Certainly, that word could not be "There." She imagined what her life would be like if she were no longer here, meaning existing. Maldon felt that when she was able to commit suicide, she would breathe the air of freedom for the very first time. Meanwhile, she had become a reluctant prisoner of causality and synchronicity. As these hackneyed thoughts entered her consciousness, she fell into a deep sleep on the sofa. The ambient, static noise of the chicken clucking about provided the latent, star-clustered music of her late afternoon nap. When she woke up again, the Sun had donned a moonless, unilluminated, incomprehensible dusky hat, pretending to the be the 1984 Milan Kundera version of *The Unbearable Lightness of Being*. Her bladder was full. And, un-catastrophically, she ambled asymmetrically and crookedly toward the bathroom to relieve herself. As urine from her clit provided the last drop of itself into the toilet bowl, Maldon noticed her toothbrush for the very first time. Its green teeth were pressed, facedown, in the gray teeth of her comb. They were caught in an intimate act of tenderness, affection, and seclusion. Maldon turned her eyes away briefly, as if she had intruded on a balanced caress between two inanimate lovers and their inability to be mobile enough to carve some makeshift privacy for themselves. They were stuck in this human bathroom, forced to listen to the indiscriminate human sounds of gargles, hand and face washing, shower water, farts, toilet flushes, the soundless plummeting of crumpled toilet paper, sinking threads of dental floss, lotion rubbing, and other irritable incursions that encroached upon their rapport for one another. She felt sorry for them both. She understood that perhaps these two different kinds of teeth may never experience carnal knowledge of one another, one set of teeth brushing the other set of teeth like apes picking fleas off each other's backs, but their recent familiarity and rapport and even warmth toward one another moved Maldon deeply. She found it hard to peel her eyes away from them to return to the kitchen to care for the abandoned center, Maurkice. Maurkice Pouncey, the center she named the seventh chicken after, was a football player for the Pittsburgh Steelers. Technically, his first name was LaShawn, but sometimes she called him Ice. He was drafted into the NFL in 2010. Maldon didn't care how well he played his position; she was hyper-pleased that he was 138 kilograms, or over three-hundred pounds. With Neptune on his period and being heavily iron-deprived and all, he was the go-to chicken. Maurkice was still considered an active player, but after this dinner he wouldn't be; Maldon was pretty sure of that. She walked back to the kitchen, divided him into thighs, wings, drumsticks, neck, back, breasts, heart, liver, gizzard, feet, and tail. She threw half of him into the oven with some chopped up broccoli and the rest of him into a pot to make broth. Maurkice would be playing a different kind of football in both Maldon's and Neptune's stomachs, and it was called self-enlisted natural iron supplement, freshly baked for any previous rookie of the year. Later, when Neptune tasted his feet, she could tell that he had either broken his ankle or injured it. True to form, in 2013 Maurkice Pouncey tore his ACL and MCL, and in 2015 he broke his fibula during a game against the Green Bay Packers. By eating the objects of one's fixation, Maldon realized that she could learn a lot about the uncensored history of their anatomical composition and possibly the psychology of their soul. But is knowing someone's broken tendencies in America's most perverse version of bullfighting the ultimate game changer of all game changers? Perhaps not. Perhaps it was only Maldon's way of finding virtue in insignificant things as everything else about life seemed to repel her and stirred unfounded leaflets of ontological revolt in her. She recalled a few of those revolts and their antipodes. She recalled, before slaughtering Doak Walker, the Heisman Winner, a profound conversation they had had.

MALDON: Before you go, I have an aching question.
DOAK: What is it?

MALDON: What was the probability of this?

DOAK: What was the probability of what?

MALDON: There were three pitch-black football stadiums in the middle of Florida. Three thousand white men and one black man were inserted in the first stadium. In the second stadium, 30,000 white men and one black man were thrust inside. Thirty white men and one black man were pushed into the last stadium. One hole the size of a man's head was carved out of each stadium, permitting only one man to emerge at a time. In all three scenarios, a black man was the first to emerge. This was repeated an infinite number of times, yet each black man was always the first to exit the hole. What was the probability of this?

DOAK: I don't know, Salt. Arithmetic isn't my strength. Football is.

MALDON: I know.

DOAK: Why did you ask?

MALDON: Jung, the Swiss psychoanalyst, who was fascinated with the structure and dynamics of the psyche, like I am, mentions in his book *Synchronicity* the following experiment: "You take three matchboxes, put 1,000 black ants in the first, 10,000 in the second and 50 in the third, together with one white ant in each, shut the boxes, and bore a hole in each of them, small enough to allow only one ant to crawl through at a time. The first ant to come out of each of the three boxes is always the white one."[1] The chances of this actually occurring are enormously improbable. Even in the first two instances, the probability is deliberately calculated to 1: 1000 x 10,000, which shows that such a concurrence is to be anticipated merely in 1 instance out of 10,000,0000, says Jung. Yet it does happen, as demonstrated by the experiment.

DOAK: I understand. Black men do matter. We white men have statistically made it nearly impossible for black men to succeed in this world. To come out first. Without grave consequences.

MALDON: Death, usually. Which I understand. No longer an experiment, given the extreme degree of improbability, in a collectively high number of white men, black men do come out first.

DOAK: As demonstrated. May I die now?

Maldon understood that American Football, led by the NFL, is, like killing chickens, a concussed, fatal business. The top male players do get paid well, generally in the millions, and their highly prized coaches, naturally, also make millions. But it comes with a price. The head goes first, concussed, and the rest of the body falls apart after. It is a sport that celebrates violence and rewards violence. Injuries are categorized in two groups: head and non-head. The head is, generally, more fatal. But if a healthy, capable athlete is paralyzed from the neck or waist down, it's physiologically and ontologically fatal too.

---

1 Jung, C.G: *Synchronicity: An Acausal Connecting Principle.* p. 60; Princeton University Press, Princeton, New Jersey.

SATURN: This illness business, Salt, it's a funny one.

MALDON: How so?

SATURN: It makes me feel out of sorts, like concussed.

MALDON: Oh no.

SATURN: You don't know what it's like to be a black wom-
            an and sick.

MALDON: Are all of your defense systems down?

SATURN: If I go out in the world like this, they're going to
            destroy me.

MALDON: Who?

SATURN: White men!

MALDON: Help me understand.

SATURN: I know you have a football team of chickens you
            are decapitating, so we'll go with that. Most foot-
            ball empires are ruled by white men and, like the
            prison system, it's a business that benefits white
            men the most. Both sports, prison and football,
            are not only lucrative but also lethal. Some say
            that death makes money, but death really makes
            money for white men. You would think that
            death is an impartial, objective adjudicator, but
            this couldn't be more untrue for colored folks
            like me. See, when black men die, neurological-
            ly (the force behind their existence and power),
            the supremacy of white men increases. While
            prison incarcerates black men physically (liter-
            ally), football incarcerates black men cerebral-
            ly. In the sports of violence, violence produces
            rippling effects. For instance, it's not enough
            that black men become primary neurological

victims of both sports; they also make (black) women develop neurological impairment and disfigurement too. Ray Rice who knocked out, World Heavyweight Champion style, his then-fiancée, Janay, in the elevator and dragged her, yes, dragged her like a dirty trash bag out of the garbage bin called Revel casino—she married him, yes, married him after the assault. If this marriage wasn't a neurological side effect from a concussed business called football, what was it? Ray semi-apologized for punching his wife like a boxing bag, but if a man has been retarded out of his intelligence by being pummeled over and over by the punching gloves of football for millions of spectators, does his apology even make sense? Does he have enough reasoning ability left in him to apologize?

MALDON: Obviously, he couldn't blame white men for punching his wife since they never "threw" the punch.

SATURN: But, Salt, white is a color of both visibility and invisibility. Visible when exhibiting power; invisible when dispelling blame. If black men are incarcerated, how do women receive neurological damage if these men were not around to inflict it? Because they are not around, their absence produces a counterpunch that is more powerful than an actual punch. When black men enter the prison system, women experience what kind of neurological injuries? They too live in a concussed state: welfare, gangs, shoot-outs, drugs, malnutrition in education, food, socialization, broken homes, orphanages, depression— you name it. They have it. By giving themselves all the power, white men create a Walmart for social, psychological, and intellectual pain for all those who subsist under them. If you shop at Walmart for a fleabag, shop for a black girl, me, without a father at the white men's Walmart too.

MALDON: We call this democracy, but perhaps it's best depicted as fascism dressed as capitalism.

SATURN: Yes, yes, exactly.

MALDON: If you put hot water into a kettle, boil it up, add mint droplets to it, pour it into a bowl, and inhale it, it should clear your head up.

SATURN: Girl, you just missed the point. I am clear here but not there. But I'll add some eucalyptus oil to the kettle.

Just like that, Maldon exited her phone conversation with her faraway lover, Saturn. Even a minor cold made her black lover feel like she had played national football on a wet, cold day in New England. Maldon was drawn to Saturn because of her cosmic dust and her enigmatic photochemical cycle. Being in her presence also made her feel existential, as if suicide could wait. Although it took Saturn, an oblate spheroid, twenty-nine years to orbit the Sun, it didn't take this beautiful Cronian long to orbit Maldon. Only a few weeks or even less. Planet Saturn had courted her by walking and escorting her to an evening class that Maldon taught at Westerlund. Even after she had

gotten used to the Westerlund's campus and could geographically navigate herself fully and painlessly to class without
getting lost, the planet would still chivalrously bodyguard her.
During that short five-minute walk to an ugly building called
Spike, she could feel her heavy heart growing lighter and lighter. The air was both crisp and moist. Even under the heavy
blanket of the night, she could feel Saturn's electric current
passing through her. Even on days when the planet felt quite
yellow and pale from her ammoniac upper atmosphere, her
interior was densely and intensely thermal, with her core at
ten-thousand Celsius on a typical day, and was able to outcompete the Sun at least twice in his radiance. Maldon felt warm,
luminous, and protected under her embrace.

Ψ

It had been a long, rapturous day for both Neptune and Maldon. They had spent the day Uubering to the hospital and bookstore. At Alpha Centauri, a different hospital from Alpha UMi Aa (but not too far from it; after all, it was a city of hospitals, a cluster of them in a very small area), they met Maldon's cardiologist for the first time. While in the waiting room, Planet Neptune noticed the names of the different cardiologists: Dr. Horchata Semifreddo, Dr. Toasted Meringue, Dr. Double Ginger, Dr. James Mascarpone, Dr. Monkey Bread, Dr. An Weekday. Reading the names of the board, her stomach began to growl like a bear, and she wondered if this mouthwatering, succulent state was common with patients who visited Alpha Centauri or if it was just an isolated incident. When she filled out her chart on a clipboard, she almost became mildly confused that it was not a pastry menu. The chart instead asked her the frequency of her chest pain, nausea, shortness of breath, etc. Although she was on a gluten-free diet, she was grateful not to be allergic to her cardiologist, Dr. Mascarpone, whom she liked seconds after meeting him. The opposite of a soft Italian cream cheese, he was tall, and his long limbs were like daddy longlegs, which allowed him to move effortlessly around the room. He held his stethoscope around his neck like a necklace and when he moved the stethoscopic pearl from his neck to her chest to spyglass into the sonic Morse code of her throbbing, cardiovascular existence, she felt like he could decode her and, somehow, she trusted him to do so. He didn't need to be Alan Turing, the British homosexual logician and cryptanalyst who committed suicide with cyanide, to decrypt her: she was easy to read. Could he decipher the most obvious, that her soul was homeless? Her existence throbbing with pain.

Before he entered, she had been studying the posters in the examination room. One was printed in large yellow letters: *Let's talk about angina.* Below the words was a heart that looked more like a crimson liver with veins. The rest of the text read: "*angina may be a symptom of coronary heart disease. People experience angina in different ways: uncomfortable pressure, squeezing, heaviness, or burning in the chest; pain in the shoulder, arm, back, neck, or jaw; feeling faint, tired, out of breath, or as if they have heartburn;*" and she realized that when she was teaching at Westerlund, she had been experiencing all of this, especially the last bullet point, "*limiting activities to avoid angina.*" She only taught one class a week, and it was only a two-hour class, but she spent at least sixty-plus hours in a resting state.

⟩

When she entered the bathroom, droplets of blood from her uterus fell into the toilet bowl. Nineteen days ago, her nine-day period had ended, and now it had rejuvenated itself again. "A flower is born in my toilet bowl," Maldon whispered out loud to herself. A voice, her own, unrecognizable even to her, also bloomed red, leaving no scars of its verbal menstruation. To replenish her iron deficit, Maldon strolled into the kitchen to microwave Maurkice Pouncey, but when she opened the refrigerator, most of him was gone. Neptune was also in the kitchen pouring himself a cup of coffee she'd made for her. In fact, all of Maurkice was gone. What was left of him hadn't decalcified.

NEPTUNE: Sorry, Salt, I can order you something and have it delivered to us.

MALDON: I think I'll put an end to the quarterback.

NEPTUNE: She isn't very fat.

MALDON: And neither is Jerry Rice.

NEPTUNE: But he is taller.

MALDON: We're just going to have to eat Erin Rodgers, Nep.

NEPTUNE: Who will lead the team?

MALDON: I will. Could you take out the trash? The one in the bathroom too.

NEPTUNE: I can't believe you're asking me to.

148

MALDON: I've done it at least five or six times since we have been here. I have never asked you once to do it.

NEPTUNE: I didn't know.

Silently, Neptune blew off some liquid hydrogen from his noseless nostril and proceeded to take the trash out. Midway through the task, as she opened the door leading to the backyard, he noticed the trash bin tipping over. She rushed immediately inside and slammed the door.

NEPTUNE: The trash can is tipped over.

MALDON: Nice job.

NEPTUNE: I didn't do it. Do you think it was the wind?

MALDON: So the wind did it. You should mention it to Airbnb so they will clean it up.

NEPTUNE: I'm definitely not going to clean it.

MALDON: They should have someone come weekly to take the trash to the curb.

NEPTUNE: They do charge us obscenely for cleaning services, but I don't see any cleaning.

To give herself some respite from her research and to relieve Maldon from her menstrual despair, Planet Neptune dragged her to the city center of Alpha Tau to see the botanical garden. When they arrived there in a blue Uuber, the garden appeared before them like a glass spaceship designed to house a factory of intransigent women who would one day be trained and converted into prophetesses for post dynasties before the forgotten era of Facebook, Alibaba, Amazon, etc. The dome-shaped exterior had ridges bent into a million micro-triangles. They triangulated fearlessly as if latched onto each other for life. The

botany architecture housed a few dozen neophyte plants, neophyte as in young, that were also epiphytic in their bromeliad-
ic tendencies. These ferns and air plants fascinated Neptune
to no end. He wished he was epiphytic too. Except for her,
it would be his ability to grow, non-parasitically, onto another
planet, such as Jupiter. Neptune had always been quite fond of
her, but she remained utterly indifferent to his existence.

Near a demarcated rectangular plot of land where the tulips
were blooming and tossing their heads against the backdrop
of a well-groomed, highly manicured patch of grass, Maldon
noticed a narrow aquarium the size of a full tower computer
case. Six inches of the aquarium's lower body were stuffed into
soil. Above and in the soil, a family of plants and flowers of ge-
raniums, marigolds, dahlia, peonies, rhododendron, and chry-
santhemums grew and bloomed. Near the aquarium stood a
small, beautiful child. Her eyes were luminous and bright, like
Vega from the northern constellation of Lyra. Her eyes were
only twenty-five light-years from the Sun, but Planet Neptune
noticed her immediately.

NEPTUNE: Where were you born, child?

But the brightest star in the universe did not reply immediately.
Both of her parents appeared immediately beside her.

CATHOLIC: Hi, I am Catholic, and this is my husband,
              Ethos.
NEPTUNE: I am Planet Neptune.
CATHOLIC: Please forgive us. We are a little overpro-
              tective.

NEPTUNE:	I understand. This is your bright daughter then?
ETHOS:	Yes, her name is Laurel. And—
MALDON:	I am Maldon Interstellar.
CATHOLIC:	Nice to meet you both.
MALDON:	Likewise. It is a beautiful day, isn't it?
CATHOLIC:	Certainly.
NEPTUNE:	Marvelous. Do you have more of these bright things around the corner?
CATHOLIC:	She's our only one.
ETHOS:	We lost a couple of them a decade or so ago.
MALDON:	I'm sorry for your loss.
NEPTUNE:	It's an exquisite garden, isn't?
CATHOLIC:	Indeed.
MALDON:	What brings you here?
CATHOLIC:	Her grandmother died, and she wanted to be buried here. We thought, as a reprieve from all the funeral arrangements . . . Besides, Laurel loves botany—
ETHOS:	And psychoanalysis.
NEPTUNE:	They love it that young?
MALDON:	She must be precocious.
CATHOLIC:	She is.

Before they departed, they saw some orchids and walked across the enclosed woman-made bridge, which hosted only one waterbird, a goose, who had stuck her bill under her armpit and slept the afternoon away. Maldon took some pictures of some bonsai and some pictures of Rocky Mountain juniper, *juniperus scopulorum*, and some pink cotton lamb's ears, *Stachys lavandulifolia*. She even snapped a picture of the different elongated shadows cast by the trellis of poles, beams, lights, and moss above them.

Somewhere near all of these ravishing beauties, Maldon was a million miles away. She was thinking about a possible infection entering her bloodstream, infecting her mechanical valve. A valve that was not made of metal as she had been led to believe. Pyrolytic carbon. Its sewn annuloplasty ring had a cuff made of Teflon, which made her think of the 16-quart pot she often used to make *canh khoai*. It was far from being as accurate as possible—a pot made out of Dacron or polyester—but the logic did pass through her like a semitruck through a desolate city.

By the time they arrived home it was dark and foreboding. Planet Neptune was on the phone with his gynecological mother on the front porch, and Maldon was inside packing. The nurse who had booked the appointment for them had told Neptune to pack a pair of clothes overnight for Maldon in case the angiogram went awry. Just as Maldon had been busy taking photographs of botany, the angiogram tech would be photographing her arteries by dyeing them the color of the sky or, as Planet Neptune had so ingeniously depicted, "she would be coloring like a coloring book and painting your heart cobalt so they could see the structure of your vessels." She imagined her heart blue like the sea of her jeans, like her thin sapphire windbreaker, and like her blue backpack. It would be the first time in her life when her heart was ebulliently and extravagantly color-coordinated with the wardrobe and the content of her psychosis, like Picasso's navy-blue period. The botany excursion had drained Maldon quite oppressively. She tried to rest on the sofa, but the chemical from the sunscreen she had applied to protect her skin from ultraviolet radiation had colluded with the Sun, and the two of them had worked in tandem to sneak into her eye sockets. As the sunscreen, sunlight, and tears attempted to homogenize or even start a book club together, they began to burn inside her. With her eyes immolating, she could not rest or fall asleep. In the midst of her restlessness, Planet Neptune screamed from outside, banging the front door like two uncontrollable cymbals.

NEPTUNE: Fuck me. It's a raccoon, and he's s so big.

MALDON: You're seventeen times bigger than the Earth, and you are terrified of a fox wearing a mask?

NEPTUNE: It's a raccoon, and I actually thought it was the wind.

MALDON: I don't think the wind has any paws.

NEPTUNE: He has a huge butt too. He was couched low. I hate him. His casual attitude toward me like he didn't care. A raccoon is just an overgrown fearless rat. That's what he is.

MALDON: He can't be worse than a possum.

NEPTUNE: Ughh. He was disgusting. At any rate, I spoke to my mother.

MALDON: I could tell.

NEPTUNE: She said to just take Coumadin. It's silly to get a lower quality valve.

The most difficult thing about slaughtering Erin Rodgers, Maldon's favorite quarterback, was the history behind the birth of her stardom.

QB: I don't want to die.

MALDON: I do.

QB: Well, if only we could exchange handshakes.

MALDON: If only I could be you.

QB: Everyone wants to be me, but they don't know the pain behind the passion.

MALDON: I know. I have studied you.

QB: What have you learned?

MALDON: They slighted you earlier in your career. During the draft. You watched everyone get picked and selected by big places. You waited and waited. In that terrible room.

QB: Quite anxiously. I watched the room empty out like a doctor draining the carcass of an animal.

MALDON: You watched and then you waited.

QB: It was humiliating.

MALDON: And you understood it as part of your humility.

QB: What if happiness isn't a moment but a span of time?

MALDON: They are ready to slaughter you like I am ready to thrash you because of one bad season.

QB: Even great players can't win all the time. My grandpa, Favre—

MALDON: Well, you watched him play and play while they benched you. Yet, day in and day out you train and drill yourself like no one has before. Your work ethic is phenomenal.

QB: I had no other choice. I knew Grandpa would retire eventually. Could you not slaughter me?

MALDON: I can't. I am hungry.

QB:	My paycheck is large. I can feed you.
MALDON:	I want to eat death. I am practicing eating death so that when death comes for me, I will know how to eat him.
QB:	I see.
MALDON:	Besides, a football team in hell needs a quarterback.
QB:	Who are you replacing me with?
MALDON:	A nobody.
QB:	Nobody who?
MALDON:	Joe Montana.
QB:	You're kidding.
MALDON:	I am not.
QB:	But he's still alive. Retired, but still alive.
MALDON:	I butchered him in my previous stay at another Airbnb.
QB:	What do you call a chicken serial killer?
MALDON:	Human.
QB:	What was it like obliterating him?
MALDON:	There are two dreams I had that you should know before I—
QB:	Crush me.
MALDON:	Yes. In the first dream, a man lies in a hospital bed. A sword was stabbed into his heart. After he dies, he wakes up briefly to say "hello" and then goes back to dying.
QB:	That man has a good sense of humor.
MALDON:	He does. Doesn't he?
QB:	Is the second as comedic?
MALDON:	It's different. In this dream, I had given my

driver the wrong directions, and she had to
make a U-turn. I kept telling her that she must
make a U-turn, so eventually she did. In the
same dream, a man is murdered execution-style
with a nail. They nailed his forehead to a door
that was high off the ground, and when they
executed him, due to the consistent nature of
gravity and the way the human body without
a functioning head unravels itself, the force of
his fall pushed the door open, and his body,
still in a stiff, vertical position, plunged down a
slanted slope, and his head with a nail still in it
was dragged down to the cement floor, where
the nail made bloody indentation marks as if he
were drawing and creating meaningless, unread-
able symbols like the needle of a protractor, the
protractor being his body.

QB: Why have you been killing men off in your
         dreams?

MALDON: Is it men or is it me?

The earliest football ever conceived had been manufactured by
exploiting pig bladders. When Maldon baked and dressed Erin
Rodgers she had chopped off Erin Rodgers' thighs and wings
so that she ultimately took the shape of a football. She stuffed
her pseudo pigskin, or rather fowlskin, with fish sauce, one cup
of white rice, four dates, and one pound of Humboldt cheese.
(It wasn't the Marieke Gouda one that Wisconsin was known
for, but it was fashionable enough for the two of them to consume.) When she sewed the prolate spheroidic Erin Rodgers

up, she used white butcher's twine to bear a resemblance to the symbolic painted marks on any rubber or synthetic footballs and to augment nocturnal visibility for the voracious Neptune when he fumbled in the dark for midnight snacking. After all, Erin Rodgers had been, many times, the backup quarterback for the Green Bay Packers and eventually their quarterback.

⊙

The morning of Maldon's angiogram appointment at Alpha UMi Aa, Maldon was bleeding profusely, and Planet Neptune had woken up early, an ungodly seven a.m. early, to put on the kettle in the shape of a fowl (it had a spout that was its beak, a round body as if capable of holding liquid eggs, a lid that could crow if one begged it to), an aquamarine hen, and softly declared, "See, I don't struggle to wake up if I have a commitment. Or if it's for someone else." When the kettle came to a hissing boil, it shrieked like it had been murdered by Maldon, but it hadn't been murdered at all. Quite the opposite, in fact. With a shrieking sound that dominated the kitchen, it seemed more like the kettled hen was trying to assassinate the room. Maldon and Neptune had run out of spring water and were boiling the water to make it drinkable.

When the ultrasonographer placed the gel against her left breast to measure the area of the blood that flowed back into her heart, she felt as if the ultrasonographer was rubbing chicken broth onto her—bones, connective tissues, collagen. Forced to lie on her left side, she could see on the ultrasound screen two flaps flapping back and forth. She told the ultrasonographer that she thought the way they moved looked as if two aliens were having a thumb war inside her mitral valve.

The anesthesiologist shaved her pubic area with an electric blade. In her mind, when she told her she must do this, Maldon had imagined a basin, a razor blade, some foam, and water from a pitcher being poured by the cardiologist the way anointing oil was decanted onto Aaron's cranium in Leviticus 8:12 to consecrate him. Before they dyed her heart blue, the anesthesiologist fed her Frenadol and some kind of relaxant. Frenadol, she learned much later, was seventy-nine (an arbitrary number) times stronger than morphine. She responded to the high dose by puking all the hospital food into a wastebasket. After the procedure, they delivered her salmon made of cardboard sprinkled with dead thyme and mixed fruits of slivered cantaloupe and pineapple cubes, but they all went out of her the way Avicii exited the music world and life. On the Uuber drive back to the Airbnb, Maldon noticed how luminescent the Sun was. The way light fell onto the acacia leaves, once planted in Whangarei, before bouncing back into her eyes, made everything hyperreal and verdant. When the Uuber paused in between traffic lights, the temporary shade provided by the red horse chestnut gave her a momentary reprieve from the thought of suicide. She even embraced the small ways in which the acacias opened majestically and spread themselves like well-behaved and well-queued caterpillar legs. In some distant memory, she recalled, before the Frenadol took hold of her consciousness, how unbearably beautiful life was. She recalled, before fading away, how the saline drips traveled through her bloodstream the way the air bubbles inside the thin plastic tubes made their way into a house builder's hand. Architects used their high-precision spirit level bubble ruler to measure the quality of their symmetry, but perhaps her body had used the air bubble from her saline drip to measure the hidden properties of her pending life.

☽

In the evening of her recuperation, after a long day at the hospital, the long wait from the hospital's high incidence of heart attack, Planet Neptune took her frustration out by biting Maldon's head off. They sat uncomfortably in silence at the dining table while the remaining chickens cooed and gawked at them the way bystanders gawked at the Cathedral when Notre Dame was incinerated. If the silence continued at an inconspicuous rate of intense tension, the chickens might even gather like a church choir around Maldon and Neptune to break out into sonic avenues of "Ave Maria." But at the heart of it, the half dozen chickens behaved more like coordinated Easter terrorists in the midst of their buffet queue in a Sri Lankan hotel: nonchalantly chilling and holding replenishable plates. At any rate, they had eaten all of Erin Rodgers in the early morning of their awakening, so protein-deprived Neptune wanted to boil her some eggs. However, Maldon wanted fried eggs instead. The egg that Planet Neptune fried for her looked like a yellow galaxy, the yolk being the Sun, spilling all over the distant stars of the egg white. The planet even boiled Maldon some perfect eggs. When Planet Neptune peeled one egg for her and placed it on the table with salt and pepper, Maldon thought: a planet peeling a planet to feed one human mouth. They had planned to go to the gay bar in downtown Alpha

Tau, but they had naively underestimated the severity of Maldon's convalescence.

NURSE: If you see blood pooling, place pressure on her wrist and dial 9-1-1.

NEPTUNE: I don't have any hands.

NURSE: Sit on her.

NEPTUNE: That's a lot of hydrogen, helium, and methane on her.

NURSE: That's better than her bleeding out.

NEPTUNE: How long can she bleed?

NURSE: Without pressure, she'll die in fifteen minutes.

To avoid the unknown, their night was forced to have the consistency of Maldon stabbing Cheetos with a fork, eating, bleeding, texting, and doing everything with her left hand, and Neptune roaming about doing chores around the Airbnb: washing dishes, washing a load of towels, packing in preparation for their relocation to their next Airbnb, etc. Maldon, deprived of these exciting tasks, was obligated to watch with watering mouth and envious eyes. Sitting on the sofa, with her arteries vulnerable, Maldon thought how easy it would be to slip into a state of unconsciousness if she yanked the bandage off and gently stabbed her exposed access wound with a pen. It would be like God holding a .44 Magnum or a machine gun to her head and clicking. In a quarter of an hour, she could be the chickens she had so silently eviscerated.

⊙

The day they left the Airbnb, Maldon brought all the chickens with her, or whatever remained of her not-so-fancy quarter-back-less football team. Without a proper leader, the auto-idiosyncratic chickens behaved like anarchistic, non-revolutionary fluffy bowling balls in their exquisite monarchless despair. They packed up everything. A bucket. Two jugs of water. Their books and toothbrushes and toothpaste. Their winter articles and coats. Their notepads and research papers. Their bottles of fish sauce and root-shaped ginger. They opened and unopened all the doors, cabinets, drawers. They checked up and down, obsessively double-checking to make sure they left nothing behind. They even turned over the bedcovers. They packed it all in the intergalactic-sized blue luggage that Planet Neptune had brought all the way from Los Angeles. The kind driver, a male version of Margaret Cho, helped him stuff it all into the enormous trunk of his vehicle. Maldon did all the lifting with one arm. Planet Neptune gathered the three remaining hens and three cocks into his hydrogenic upper atmosphere and stuffed them into the back seat of the Uuber. For being so chivalrous with them, the planet even offered the driver a case of Bell's Lager beer from Kalamazoo, Michigan. He responded by waving a dismissal embrace, saying, "Perhaps after I drop you both off?" Before they left, Planet Neptune texted the host that during his energetic Poseidon-endowed sleep, his faint ring system had knocked the lamp over, and now it was broken and shattered.

During the long drive to their new Airbnb, Maldon read Hemingway's *Death in the Afternoon*, and Neptune gazed out of the long, isolating, desolate landscape of Alpha Tau. They crossed two aqueducts, three dams, two construction sites, and escaped a dozen roadblocks. The ride made her bilious and seasick as if they were on a boat, but this vehicle was no yacht. Then Maldon recalled the planet reciting her semi-lucid echolalia, "'They narcoticized me. They narcotized me. They narcotized me.' That's what you kept on repeating." She reread the line on page fifty-four of Hemingway: "True mysticism should not be confused with incompetence in writing which seeks to mystify where there is no mystery but is really only the necessity to fake to cover lack of knowledge or the inability to state clearly. Mysticism implies a mystery and there are many mysteries; but incompetence is not one of them." The nausea came with or without the bullfighting. Without much thinking, she gripped one cock's feathery exterior and, by pure defeat, plucked one feather from him. "You don't mind, do you?" she asked. He turned his fowl-y head around in alarm as she earmarked the page with her makeshift bookmark. He didn't seem to agree, but he didn't really have a choice. She begged the driver to pull over, and when he pulled over, she stepped out and puked up her breakfast: fried egg, boiled egg, moon cake, a glass of water—a constellation of a split dream between reality and a half-vomited life. When she stood up from puking, she studied the whiteness of the summer dress her mother had made for her and the scarf that Planet Mercury had gifted to her after his brief travel to Pakistan and stared at the desolation of alfalfa mixed with the calm despondency of the rice field. She noticed the postman strolling by in the grass with his mail stroller. If he wasn't wearing his postman uniform, it would look as if he were carting a baby. She liked the idea of him there. It was comforting and almost dis-enabling. She couldn't seem to put a finger on it, like he wasn't supposed to be there, but somehow or someway God forced him to be there, be that lonesome blue figure in blue prose on that green field of wretchedness. A rabbit hopped into her view, lingering lightly. Its arms tucked up, a softness to the bastard's petite hyraxity that made him unbearably beautiful there. Instead of declaring the nonexistent nature of her pregnancy, it wagged its V-shaped ears. Rabbits had a shearing susceptibility and defenselessness about them, she had always felt, but they chewed grass, and this herbivorous state of consumption somehow made them pseudo-impervious to harm and abuse. She stared down at the vomit, a nobody's art piece, immaterial and uneducational, and spoke to it: "I pull you out of me, and now you are just squatting there, useless, not moving an inch." If she wasn't still narcoticized, she might have imagined masturbatory laughter from the content's tactility. *To operate on me, they are obligated to stop my heart. They are going to stop my heart. They are stopping my heart like a stop sign,* she reminded herself. From vomit to a potential mental agenda on the list. She wiped her mouth with the scarf. In the Victorian and even post-Victorian era, paradise could last forever. One's attention span could afford it. But what about now? thought Maldon. The most important question for all modern species in the informational age was this: how long should paradise

last? And how long could she keep on eating chickens at her
current rate when she knew it was not the antidote to happiness and a game changer for genocide? I am a machine. I have
always been a machine, Maldon told herself. And now the surgeon was planning to reboot her. The next time she woke up,
she wouldn't have a new operating system. They would have
replaced and updated her memory, allowed her the supersonic
ability to travel faster. The war to sustain Darwinism was dead.
The game of the fittest was just a game, a fantasy game in a video console called material realism. Not everyone gathered their
hens and cocks to hug them before the carnage, but Maldon
did just that. But now that she was dress rehearsing her own
death, she was no longer a machine. She would soon be just
an injured animal on the grass, watching the world go by. She
thought about Planet Neptune, who had been talking loudly to
her to get her attention, but she had zoned out. Then he was
wobbling by her side. The odor of his helium. If she got any
closer to her body, and if Maldon's body were made of rubber,
he would blow her up to be a balloon. But since she was made
of human flesh, his monatomic presence became some kind
of coolant, unraveling her from a state of hyper-vertigo into a
state of esophageal repose. Like a soccer player, Planet Neptune propelled her into the Uuber vehicle with the infinitesimal
force of his head. During her emetic state, it became telepathic
later only to her that all Neptune did all along was apply his
broad atmospheric forehead to nudge the antsy, restless football team back into the Uuber. A gentler version of Zinedine
Zidane headbutting Marco Materazzi during the final minutes
of the 2006 World Cup. Gentler because the chickens were
not insulting Neptune or calling his mother an extraterrestrial

cunt. They all wanted to exit the car and waddle next to Maldon's vomit to either smell it or play with it.

Guided by his GPS and the Uuber app, Mr. Margaret Cho drove and drove. It seemed like forever before they reached their new dwelling. The female voice of the app announced, "You have arrived at 902 Achernar Drive." Maldon remembered why the language was so familiar to her: in Arabic, it bore the meaning of a tributary cul-de-sac. The driver had taken them down to the end of the river. As Mr. Cho attempted to pull into the driveway, a yelp emerged from Neptune's bluest lips.

NEPTUNE: This is not the right house.
MR. CHO: It says we are here.
NEPTUNE: This is 207 Achernar, not 902.
MR. CHO: Just keep going.
NEPTUNE: 309, 428, 708.
MR. CHO: 808, 1008
NEPTUNE: Between house number 808 and 1008, there was only grass.
MR. CHO: That's so strange. Where could it be?
NEPTUNE: Let's keep driving.

Mr. Cho made a circle around a makeshift fountain constructed of grass and concrete. In a few minutes he was back on the main street. He turned into a curved road that led straight to Rigelstar Street. The landscape around them was barren. The undeveloped land had a few sprawling houses still under construction, with text-laden manufacturer's wallpaper and stickers still glued to the exteriors. Sometimes, when the wind was just right, Maldon could see parts of the manufacturers' wallpaper flapping in the wind. Mr. Cho kept on driving. The numbers decreased before increasing.

MR. CHO: The house must be so new that it's not even on
             Google Maps.
NEPTUNE: It's fucking unbelievable. I have no idea where
             we are.
MALDON: I don't think the house exists. Maybe the host
             made a false listing.
MR. CHO: Should I keep going?
NEPTUNE: I don't know what to do.
MR. CHO: I only know how to drive so I'm just driving.
MALDON: Why don't you call the host, Nep?
NEPTUNE: Let's give it a minute. Maybe the house might
             appear like a solar eclipse.
MALDON: But the next ring of fire won't appear until July.
             It's only May.
NEPTUNE: It was just a simile, Salt. A simile!

In *The Matrix*, cyber lawbreaker and hacker Neo was found in an infinite subway station, immovable between the real world and the Matrix. Some said his pre-human integrated ontological Wi-Fi, the part of his brain where Wi-Fi was supernaturally implanted into his encephalonic stem even before his Earth DNA was born, allowed him to be in, meaning granted him access to, the station without being hooked up to a machine. By driving endlessly from one part of Alpha Tau to Alpha Mau, Maldon, Neptune, and Mr. Cho were trapped in a similar time loop without being able to dismount from their Uuber ride. The cautious, morally efficient driver could not just dump them in the middle of nowhere with their baggage still in his trunk. Then there was the metal bucket and two jugs of water and half a football team of Germanic vogels in the backseat screeching, squawking, and crying in disagreeable squeals of hysteria. Seven loops and three hours went by, and still Neptune and Mr. Cho glued their noses and eyes to the numbers as they ascended and descended and then disappeared altogether. By the late afternoon the driver was bitterly exasperated and, inevidently, Planet Neptune had a nervous breakdown. She buried his face into the warm, soft upper torso of the chicken. Maldon volunteered to help, but he shut her down as soon as she opened her mouth.

MALDON: Nep. Call the fucking host. Call him.
NEPTUNE: Alright alright.

The driver turned around, giving his phone to Neptune to insert the new info into while Neptune dialed the number using his own handheld satellite. The host told them that they were on the right street but that they must cross over to the other side. There was a gorge that bifurcated the street into north and south. They were at the cul-de-sac of the north end of the development. They must cross through several football fields of mud and bypass a forest before they could reach their Airbnb. The driver immediately shifted gears and spun on his accelerator like a man being chased by a storm of serial killers. As they bolted through the uneven road between gravel and mud, it started to rain. A few droplets here and there, as if a teenage girl had started sobbing silently and quietly and intently to herself, and then the gush and the surge spilled out. Even when the driver forced his windshield wipers to work meticulously and ravenously overtime, it could not keep up with the pluvial wrath. The chickens had stopped their squawking. Pressed together like a half dozen vanilla cream-filled donuts, they had fallen asleep. The rain was murderously beautiful, thought Maldon. The constant, sonic tapping and the way thunder just hatefully fulminated across the cloud-laden sky. When they reached the southern point of their excursion, they remained lost. Mr. Cho threw up this hands in a fit of indignation, nearly sending his phone through the windshield. Planet Neptune's bluest eyes had turned dark gray from emotion-based gravitational collapse. A hierarchy of outrage and displeasure began to transform into interstellar clusters of galaxies inside his post-thermonuclear face. Neptune, for the first time since their morning departure from the previous Airbnb, turned to Maldon for moral support.

NEPTUNE: What should we do?

MALDON: Call the host again and see if he would come to collect us.

NEPTUNE: He said he was waiting for a large delivery for his neighbor's wife, and she would kill him if he looked away for a second. They were paying him to babysit the delivery. If he failed in this small task, they would evict him from his own house and end by paying off his bank, which they literally owned.

MALDON: Look, there is the UPS man: chase after him, Nep, and ask him where the house is.

Planet Neptune slowly got out of the vehicle and ambulated softly and hesitantly. What the fuck? thought Maldon. Why doesn't he run toward him? Mr. Cho must have telepathically read her mind, or perhaps he was just as morbidly piqued as she was, because he rolled down the passenger window for her without awaiting her instructions.

MALDON: Neptune! Run! He's climbed into his truck and is driving away!

The planet leaned to his left side as she chased after the driver as if to catch the UPS man through the side mirror. Both Mr. Cho and the driver watched intently as Neptune moved the atmospheric forces around his face. Maldon was unable to read the content of his expression. When the planet climbed back into the vehicle, her curiosity multiplied an astronomical tenfold.

MALDON: So, what did he say?
NEPTUNE: He said that he also gets lost all the time. But he did say that we are near. Sort of.
MALDON: O-h m-y G-o-d!
NEPTUNE: We are fucked.
MALDON: Call him again.

Again they returned to their infinite time loop between nowhere and house numbers that increased and decreased and then disappeared altogether. Six hours had passed, yet their version of the fathomless train station remained. They begged Mr. Cho to drop them off near some tree, but he was too morally assertive to abandon them, nor did it occur to them to book a backup Airbnb. They were geographically entombed between nowhere and the middle of nowhere. From the corner of her eye, Maldon noticed an electrician in a white van with a ladder strapped on the roof.

MALDON: Chase him down, Nep! He's our human compass.

NEPTUNE: He's just a construct of our delusion!

As the planet had predicted, the man did not know a book from a roll of toilet paper. He was just as clueless. Mr. Cho noticed another man parked near the edge of a lake.

MR. CHO: He looks like he knows.

NEPTUNE: Let's ask him.

MALDON: We're all desperate. So terribly desperate.

Mr. Cho drove up to the stranger.

MR.CHO: Do you know where 902 Achernar Drive is?

STRANGER: Let me see.

Maldon watched the man plug the address into his GPS. Her eyes grew wider and wider.

MALDON: He doesn't know. Fuck. He doesn't know. He's plugging in the address as we've been doing. Let's keep going.

They abandoned him. The man without emotional coordinates. The man who was helpless without digital communication. The man whose primary compass only committed itself to a monogamous relationship with Google Maps. The driver drove and drove. And, as if it was a sign from God, a semi, the biggest commercial truck with an elongated ass, descended from the southern part of a hill. It may have been hunger and desperation that made them think for a split second that she, sitting on her high mechanical horse with eighteen rubber legs, would be able to unwind them from a geographical time loop.

⊙

In the golden field of the late afternoon, after the accident, Maldon wore a tragedy rehearsal dress for an authentic, American-made calamity. She was wearing this dress even though she could have been naked, barren, and forlorn. Near death, she found the meaning of existence and life: immortality is only a chair. Fame is just a table she would want to dine on if she could serve herself. The accident had crushed some of her ribs, but the ribs hadn't punctured her yet.

Before reaching the tree, flashes of the accident spasmed like strobe lights across her vision. When the semi descended upon them, half of the football team, like syncopated swimmers, woke up one by one from their soporific stupor and began squawking and cawing all at once. One would think that if one woke up, the others would eventually wake up, but rarely in such simultaneous succession. However, the science of emulation and imitation indicated otherwise, a counter-narrative that produced grave consequences. In their robust awakening, they must have sent each other gallinaceous Morse code or some type of telepathic mental memo that life was too short to spend sleeping and hibernating. The message must have been quite persuasive because when one woke up, the others joined. It was a choir of chickens after all. The cacophony of their unpleasant musicality startled Mr. Cho, who broke from his concentration on the road, shifted his eyes away from the semi, and turned his head around in reflex in an involuntary response to the source behind the meteoric commotion.

As the law of motion and contingency implied, Mr. Cho's vehicle logically and effortlessly kissed the front wheel of the semi as the semi driver attempted to evade him by rotating her wheel swiftly, but the impact was acute and grave. The car made several revolutions in the air before landing on its wheels. Mr. Cho, the driver, died instantly when he flew through the windshield. The constant motion of climbing in and out of the car to ask for directions, the unclicking and clicking of the seat belts, and the maddening, incensed, distinct sense of displacement and adrift-ness may have disrupted his lifelong pattern of prioritizing safety over everything else; despite how devoted he was to the ritual, the one time he failed to do it, it became fatal for him. As for Planet Neptune, he was also in the front seat of the vehicle. However, out of a protective impulse for Maldon and the chickens, during impact he had redirected his hydrogen and methane outward to supernaturally cushion and shield them in a methanic cocoon embrace, one he would like to call "his atmospheric phenomenality." The re-directing of his planetary power to inoculate and fortify others left her vulnerable to the law of chance. This law was unforgiving. The accident crushed him, leaving her gorgeous circular skull a perverse, morphed aftermath of unsupported ugliness: an ugliness called ellipticity. No longer rotund and possibly attractive as before, the entire universe responded by being remarkably offended. In a galactic offensive against this aesthetical annexation of the entire cosmic makeup, a visual hostility against Planet Neptune's sudden hideousness (though, in actuality, it wasn't hideous, just as the Supernova 1987A, or Bode's Galaxy, would never be considered hideous or unsightly or even repugnant; however, when things that were once considered circular no longer are, the only appropriate linear response to the new distortion is to call it a monstrosity), an advocate from the Sombrero Galaxy, whose primary vocation was to preserve the aesthetic and authentic nature of the universe, was teleported to Alpha Mau to zap the pulchritude-injured Planet Neptune from the Uuber. A medical interplanetary helicopter, also known as an extraterrestrial ambulance, also arrived from Sculptor Galaxy to transport Planet Neptune to galaxy NGC 1512 in constellation Horologium for an emergency face-lift operation where an extragalactic plastic surgeon from NGC 123 also disembarked in tandem with other homeopathic, restorative, and medical officers such as nurses and assistants to fix, lift, and patch the planet out of his ghastly hideousness.

Despite the planet's sincere attempt to shield Maldon and the chickens from vehicular hurt, harm did brush them a little.

⊙

After the accident, still high on shock, the injured Maldon searched up and down for the planet, but it seemed as if he had vanished into thin air. She even bent down to gaze under the vehicle. Nothing. When she discovered pizza-faced, broken-necked, shard-infused Mr. Cho, tears fell like translucent baby lilies from her eyes onto her cheeks. Half of the vehicle's windows were shattered or broken, and debris had been jettisoned onto the pastoral earth like some half-hearted Helen Frankenthaler painting. The chickens had fled the scene of the accident like guilty inmates. The desolation and miles of nothingness. Maldon was alone against the bucolic landscape of Alpha Mau in the middle of nowhere. Except for the blue sky. And a white oak standing unaided and unaccompanied like Emily Brontë after her midday walk on the moor. And except for the semi, which had tilted and fallen into a bed of wet grass like a white elephant on its side at an incline. Since the semi driver had fallen flat on the driver's side, it was unlikely that she would be able to open the driver's door. The grass was an added door that boxed and sealed her in. If she weren't injured, she could have pulled herself up to the passenger's side, kicked the door open, and lifted herself out like a sailor from a submarine.

There was a bright breeze that made her white dress flutter. It was no summer pre-evening. The cloud had shifted grayly as if it had been traveling inside J. M. W. Turner's painting with an obvious, overstated title, *Snow Storm: Steam-Boat off a Harbour's Mouth*. The painting depicted a vessel off the English coast being ambushed by a storm as it tried to persist, to shift, and to force itself out of Mother Nature's turbulent embrace. Thus, in close psychic proximity to the art piece, the sky naturally felt heavy and cryptic. The dismally cold climate was slowly traveling and unraveling itself into her immune system, breaking her down second by second on a microscopic level. The high adrenaline post-accident had kept the frigidity at bay, but now that she had time and was calmer, the cold had self-invited itself into her body. Vapor emitted from Maldon's mouth as if she had suddenly become a chronic smoker. Taking another sweep around the semi-crushed, semi-damaged Uuber, re-inspecting for a semi-existent Planet Neptune, Maldon found the cold metal bucket and one jug of water still intact. The bucket, like the jug, lay on its side, half of its round mouth kissing the grass. With only one hand that could function, she contemplated how she might be able to carry it to the white oak tree, with the primary aim of making it her burial ground. Turning the jug onto its bottom, she uncapped the lid with her left hand and lifted the jug to place it in the bucket. Halfway through the task, the pain from her broken ribs forced her to drop the thing in midair. When it flapped to the grassy ground, it nearly tipped the bucket over. Its open throat gurgled the water out, and she left it be. What was the use? she thought. She dragged the bucket as long as she could, but the bent-over nature of the body forced the ribs to jab and prod her and ultimately impale her so that she was painfully and slowly bleeding internally. In tandem with her ongoing period, Maldon was bloodstaining her existence onto the grass one unit of blood at a time: one from her asshole and the other from her uterus. If possible, she would have liked to bleed out of her wrists as well.

She wrapped her arm around the bucket and pulled it closer to her breast with her non-injured arm. At that moment she would have given anything to be closer to an American pop star. To get into that eloquent mansion of a bathtub with Whitney Houston as she overdosed on grass, daffodil, heroin. She crawled over the wet grass slowly to the tree, her arms wrapping around the bucket. The water leaped in the air but fell back down like joyful waves, and despite it being a windless day, it undulated like fabric blown in the wind. She winced in pain and then pulled the bucket as she continued to crawl. At any moment, she thought, the force of her pulling would tip the bucket over. But it never did, and she never lost the water. At one point, she cupped her fingers and scooped some of the water into her mouth. Most of it dispersed and traveled out of her fingers like liquid veins before any of it could make its way down her throat. She wasn't drinking out of thirst, just purely out of the unavoidable formality of its blatant presence.

⊙

If the accident had never occurred, Planet Neptune, Maldon, and the chickens would all be sleeping in the warm Airbnb room in a semi-large rustic house designed by the British-Iraqi architect Zaha Halid. It was a domicile that defied the logic of architectural design and re-defined the etymology of geometry and chaos. It was a type of minimalistic home that revolution-ized the informal space of antediluvian desire. Basically, it was a dwelling that had taken the shape of an inverted seashell. As Neptune wrote the last section of his research essay on Hoag's Object, Maldon would be sipping a hot glass of water, sitting near a digital fire, and finishing *Death in the Afternoon*. They would walk softly to a lake while watching the swans swimming in and out of the gloaming. It was without irony that their new, un-searchable Airbnb domicile was just one road over from the accident site. Semis did not usually make their transported pas-sage rurally. This one particular semi was shipping three titanic silos. Their Airbnb host had a neighbor. A neighbor who owned a large piece of land. The neighbor's wife was a music compos-er, and she wanted to house and play her musical instruments in each different silo. One silo to sheath a piano because she was experimenting with smothered agony: What kind of music could be drawn out of the mouth of a piano when it had been choked or asphyxiated? She wanted to manipulate ambiance and restructure the geometrical constitution of auditory space. Working on both large and small scales, she hoped to revolutionize modern music and make Mozart seem like a dimwit. If it wasn't for her obscene, astronomical passion, perhaps this accident would never have taken place.

If the accident had never occurred, and Planet Neptune hadn't been abducted or taken away for cosmetic surgery, the chickens would have gathered around Maldon like a family of owls to watch the small hailstorm that was roosting like a postman. Later, they would all watch the sky fall into a delirium of ancient ice balls as they tapped manically against glass.

If the accident had never occurred, Maldon would have been molested by a gastroenterologist who wanted to touch and feel her as she requested a consultation about Coumadin.

If the accident had never occurred, Maldon would be taking six long, deep breaths into a pulmonary machine operated by a medical soprano singer and feeling as if everything inside her was being exhumed and then reinserted back inside her. When the singer pinched her nose with a plastic clip, Maldon could have seen on the graph how her breath was measured. The graphs showed a boa constrictor being held down by the contour of an elephant whose trunk had been chopped off to make the chart feel better about its existence.

If the accident had never occurred, Maldon would be reading Julia Kristeva's *New Maladies of the Soul,* and she wouldn't be rereading this line from page seventy over and over for the next 3.6 hours: "This discrepancy takes on some well-documented forms: endless seduction *and* frigidity, an eroticization of the link with other people and the outside world *and* an untouchable autosensuality, verbal haste *and* the discrediting of speech, a erotomaniac exaltation *and* an inexorable sadness with its underlying depressive tendencies, the incitement of the father and his knowledge *and* a spasmodic, angry, and mute body that can even be morbid toward the rival, the double, the mother." She had no idea what she was reading, but if she had to phantom its possibility, it would be this possibility that if language could commit suicide, it would look and sound exactly like the declaration above.

If the accident had never occurred, Maldon and Planet Neptune and the chickens wouldn't have had dinner with an innocent couple who were crumb weepers and with whom she shared stories about fine dining, about fish being flown from Italy fresh into the desert, and about transitioning her life from its current morbid state into a life made of hemp. Would she choose a life in which she could become a marijuana merchant?

If the accident had never occurred, Maldon wouldn't have been so algorithmic and loving toward the woman who walked her dog in the twilight. She would have watched the dog pull itself away from the leash and hone its nostril against the contour of the moonlight. And so Maldon learned that the woman's dog had died not too long ago, and yet the phantom dog still clung to her leash wherever she walked. Her canine heartache projected a mirror of computed numbers onto the backs of pebbles, and if she wasn't dreaming while she unraveled across a sea of grass, she may have confused medieval bereavement with the algebraic echo of her dog's bark on every single surface she observed and encountered. She would observe that the pebbles did bark back at her. It was algebraic because the sound of the bark would emerge from various combinations of phonetic letters and numbers to re-create a "reunion of broken parts" that had once belonged to the dog and its owner. The "reunion of broken parts" came from Arabic: *al-jabr.*

If the accident had never occurred, the milkman who walked by them with two jugs bouncing against his back wouldn't have spat on them.

If the accident had never occurred, she would have heard the word "bouncy" from the lips of a straight white man, who wasn't a farmer, to describe glass noodles. Were glass noodles bouncy because they could reflect?

If the accident had never occurred, she would have taken another ride in an Uuber in which the carpenter and farmer (her driver) declared so poignantly that he hated a loud life. Maldon would recall studying his blond hair and how she wanted to comb it because it reminded her of Paul Gaugin's 1889 oil on canvas painting—those large brushstrokes—*Haymaking.* She could have imagined a life with him: small and quiet, like a haybale covered in light and cloth. Then she would realize that after climbing on his haybale very briefly, she would grow tired of his masculinity and she would need to return home again.

If the accident had never occurred, the chickens, Maldon, and Planet Neptune would be dining at a Thai restaurant on the corner of Force and Legality, where the bartender made infinite alcoholic drinks while burping every three or four minutes. The waitress re-tabled them three times, yet the air remained putrid, and the fat rice noodles were undercooked and still too fat, despite spending some time being marinated in soy sauce and overused vegetable oil.

If the accident had never occurred, somewhere Maldon could hear her lover, Planet Earth, telling her, "My darling, Maldon. What would you like for breakfast?" And she could hear herself saying: one egg yolk from the Sun, a couple spoonfuls of chocolate cookie ice cream from the Moon, and some star dust made of cocoa powder.

If the accident had never occurred, Maldon would need to contemplate two very difficult choices: on one hand, a mechanical valve and the uncertainty of bleeding out at any given moment in her life or two, the certainty of knowing that she must be operated on every decade or so. The accident resolved this impossible bind for her.

If the accident had never occurred, the following morning, the chickens would have walked and danced around in a circle, like ring-around-the-rosy, their seductive, feathery hips bouncy and in great formation as they chanted joyfully while holding hands, "Planet Neptune is a Muslim. Planet Neptune is a Muslim!"

If the accident had never occurred, on the morning of the pulmonary function exam, Maldon and Planet Neptune would have found themselves in an Uuber the following day on the longest ride of their lives. The driver urinated on the back seat and wiped it lightly with his pants. He was so fat that his girth spilled all over the back seat like an octopus with his tentacles. Even for a planet who was a formidable gas giant and could take anything astronomically repellent, this was even too much for him. Maldon could feel and hear Neptune breathing out of her other atmosphere and holding his blue ovoid head in sanity as Maldon rolled down the window in an attempt at half-hearted pulmonary escape.

⊙

By the time she made it to the tree, she was too out of breath.

Tree of life, have you been a sinner? she asked. *I am going to wash your feet now,* she tenderly informed the white oak. She crawled closer, pressed her face against its bumpy, exposed root. She could smell the post-rain dampness of the grass, the tree's arboreal verdure, and another kind of aching moistness: of life wet and dry at the same time. She pulled and pulled and tugged and tugged at her scarf with her left hand until it came off. In the whitest of all white dresses, dyed nearly half green via smearing, via crawling, she scrubbed and scrubbed, washed and washed the base of the white oak like Jesus washing the feet of his disciples. She dipped her scarf in and out of it and watched the lushness of the water falling clumsily onto the base. *You are my master, and I am your servant,* she whispered to the breath of water. She washed the tree of life tenderly while she drifted in and out of consciousness. She mumbled some incoherent makeshift biblical verses. *In an eco-world, two trees stand side by side, crucified by a lumberjack. Was it you? Or was it me?* Before losing consciousness, her eyes saw the world washing out, a bright whiteness that mimicked the sea, as if a gentle human finger had dipped into its center and caused it to ripple outward.

When she came to, she saw that the afternoon, like a frozen clock, hadn't shifted a single millimeter. The air was still. She turned her head from side to side. Then a thought occurred to her: Where was her Hemingway? Did the book fly like a peacock out of the Uuber window? Where was it now? Sleeping on grass? Walking toward her on its legless binding? How futile it all was. With all the planets orbiting around Maldon, how did she still manage to live? Even Maldon could not save herself. Her head was still pressed against the tree, the nearly empty water bucket still wobbling on the white oak's base, and the chickens were within the approximate vicinity. She cleared her throat and hollered at the hens and cocks to come over. Her voice unraveled quietly and inaudibly at first. After a few attempts, it gained depth and sound and momentum as it grew confident in its ability to declare its message: *I killed and ate over half of your football team. Come take revenge on me. Come. Peck on my wrist. Help me bleed out. Come here, please,* she begged them. They paid no heed to her. They were busy chewing the field of grass. They were tired of eating themselves and found comfort in the bucolic. They knew deep down that forsaking her was the best way to take advantage of their short life on Earth. One hen, the tailback, based on the lopsided way in which it moved, was very likely limping on one leg. Another cock, the center guard, had a quasi-isosceles shard of glass stuck to the lower left side of his chest. Yet even in pain and semi-mutilated, he had never been so happy to be peripatetic and oblivious. Here, though wobbly and injured from the accident, they roamed freely.

Who in their right mind would save their executioner?

Maldon had drifted in and out of consciousness. It was

difficult, nearly impossible, to discern what was happening to her body. Large blankets of dark clouds had formed in the murky, cloud-laden sky. It began raining again. Each blade of grass was trilling in the pluvial mist and descension. One drop of wet tear fell off the lachrymal leaves. Six chickens had by now dashed quickly toward her to seek shelter, to escape the firmament of rain and its dreamy atmospheric droplets. Within a minute, like football players during kickoff before snow fell, they bolted like balls of damp feathers and gathered under the same white oak, their makeshift umbrella. By now Maldon had lost all mobility. Even if she wanted to bleed out through the wrist by poking it with a twig, she couldn't even lift one newton of weight to do it. Their sudden ambush near her gave her the impression that they might take their revenge on her after all. By beak-stabbing her soiled white dress until she was torn open. Inevitably, they would peck her eyes out, mutilate and impale her genitals and shivering breasts with their sharp mouths until she was utterly mangled and disfigured. As they approached her, in a self-protective mode, she quietly whispered, "Please, please peck my bandage off. See that artery. Go for it. Bleed me out." As they came nearer, their alert, target-shaped eyes widened, which made her grow uneasy and apprehensive. She shut her pre-dawn eyes tight, waiting for the inevitable: to be seized and mutilated by them. Instead, they congregated themselves against her chest and stomach. Three of them climbed on her like a stubborn log and plumply sat on her like crows on an electric wire. Their warmth and their weight added pressure to her immobility. Unavoidably, inadvertently, and medically, their tenderness obstructed the bleeding. The chickens enveloped, embraced, nurtured, mother-smothered, and flocked around her with their feathery body heat as if God were placing a comforter on her as the city inside her experienced a blackout. It wasn't entirely clear to Maldon if God was the makeshift generator or the chickens. And, slowly, she drifted out of a pre-hypothermic state toward grace. Honesty is the fastest way of being in the moment, she discovered. If Maldon was honest with herself, which she was in this moment, she would admit that she loved the possibility of the unknown. She hadn't always loved it, but for the time being it was on a small list of things she prized. There was an unyielding warm regret about her life on the verge of passing away. The warm regret passed through her not like sin but like a mistake. She had been hopeless, but also mistaken. Hope for her mother was millions of miles away. Receding into the infinite, phantom depth of the cosmos. She thought how silly it was to ask permission from God to die in order to bypass her promise to stay alive until her mother died. All, all it took was a bad car accident with a semi in an Uuber to have it all. However, if she was honest with herself, Maldon realized that it was impossible to simply live this small life just for her mother. There were other things to consider, such as an umbrella that could withstand a hurricane. Moments before her death, she would tell you that she found herself excited by life. The possibility of life, not just as an act of love, but of surrendering. The chickens had taught her this. When she had imagined the worst, kindness knocked on her door. A form of forgiveness which unlocked another portal for her within herself. Kindness was the fifth dimension. An alternate universe. One which opened up from her letting go of the parallel universe. One could never know if there was the possibility of pro nihilo after ex nihilo, but one thing was certain for Maldon: the circumference of possibilities would exclude the possibility of this life, and because of the miracle of this exclusion, she realized that it was significantly better to be here rather than to be there. Wherever there may or may not be.

☽

Night was falling rapidly. Maldon could taste the rainy night air, the warmth of her chickens, the formation of dew, the small fingers of atmosphere reaching in, pulling her breath out of her singularly, methodically, and impartially. She could barely make out the impenetrable, enigmatically, and dismally minimalistic rural landscape that had imbued her. If she squinted hard, she could see the nearly invisible skid marks of the fallen semi, the small open maw of the water jug, the car a crumpled piece of paper on a picnic cloth called grass. *Death in the Evening* somewhere, maybe in a car's stomach. Maldon recalled a line, which she intentionally misquoted, from Béla Tarr's *Werckmeister Harmonies*, spoken from the innocent mouth of ambulatory Valuska: "Everything that loves is still." Does it mean that everything that is in motion hates? she contemplated rhetorically. Then, in the distilled ambient air, a tingling georgic vibration between reverberation and silence slipped its small audible note into her ears. As she slipped out of consciousness, she heard the siren wailing in the indefinite, obscure, remarkable Arcadian background. If she died, it wouldn't have mattered. She found life in this moment, and that was all that mattered. This was her fifth dimension. Her passage out of this world into her own life which was just as significant and explosive as a dead star swimming in a sea of constellations.

☉☽

EPILOGUE:

More known and celebrated for his epic, elongated, Susan Sontag-loved *Sátántangó*, Béla Tarr's best work, *Werckmeister Harmonies,* has often been overlooked by critics of its time and even contemporary thinkers of cinema. However, if one were to study Béla Tarr's opening of *Werckmeister Harmonies*, the first ten minutes—or to be exact, the first ten minutes and twelve seconds of the film—show that harmonies often do not come into being by being still. We begin to see the whirlwind of men, lubricated by artificial light and beer, as being in harmony and disharmony with the camera and the moving theater of the human breath and their human motion as Sun, Moon, planet, and distant stars. After giving birth to six films, the Hungarian director Béla Tarr was still hungry and possibly anxious in 2000 about defying the political axiom of the cosmos and the emotional language of vulnerability as he rotated his actors through Valuska (his own God and alter ego) to mirror the cosmos as tubs of beers mimicking the cosmos! And so Tarr, on his lunar and solar ascent, does not rest on the laurels of his seventh film as he warmly, though not so innocently, rotates us into his cinematic ether by declaring through his fireplace: Let me tell you about how the universe opens its eyes. Let me tell you now that the Sun doesn't move. And, if God is Valuska, then his eyes were very wide open, and Maldon wasn't dead but was very much alive through dying. Yes, it's true perhaps that all the planets in Maldon were all rotating inside, outside, and around her, and some were even retrograding or had even gone past retrograde. Perhaps in Maldon's annihilating universe, emptiness does reign. But in Béla Tarr's, the Sun is a fat, beer-bellied man wearing a striped shirt and sporting a mustache that is perhaps even too weepy for a willow tree—however, he does move by flicking his fingers while standing very still—Planet Earth is a man wearing a bowler hat and a leather jacket with his scarf around his neck (with a beard—of course Earth is a human bear!) who is being guided around by God; the Moon doesn't have any facial hair, has cheeks soft as the moonlight, wears a sweater that looks more like the texture of a wicker chair, and is forced by God to stand with hips straight but upper torso slanted to the left to make room for the Sun's flame. The viewer could see the Earth's heartbeat and a slight, nonchalant smile as if he were easily enchanted but not startled. Some say that Maldon's accident was her own version of the solar eclipse. In Tarr's version, you could hear the shoes of the Moon, Sun, Earth, and other distant stars shuffling around each other. You could hear the screeching of the floor before the bartender escorted these celestial beings out into the dark night to face the nocturnal, melancholy-charged music of Mihály Víg, whose music was so beautiful and heartbreakingly compelling that it was rumored to have caused vulnerable listeners to jump out of windows, to commit suicide afterward. You could see that life didn't come into being to be short and indifferent. You could see that life is very much about death at rest. Being at rest.

☽

Acknowledgments

The author wishes to thank the following individuals for their inherent ontological splendor and advocacy of this book: Ali Raz, Tania Sarfraz, Joanna Ruocco, Sarah Blackman, Seren Adams (S.A.), Noah Cicero, Brian Conn, Dan Waterman, and all the readers and members of the FC2 board of directors and their staff.